WICKED FRAT BOY WAYS

T0125603

Visit us at www.boldstrokesbooks.com

WICKED FRAT BOY WAYS

by

Todd Gregory

A Division of Bold Strokes Books

2017

WICKED FRAT BOY WAYS

© 2017 BY TODD GREGORY. ALL RIGHTS RESERVED.

ISBN 13: 978-1-62639-671-5

THIS TRADE PAPERBACK ORIGINAL IS PUBLISHED BY
BOLD STROKES BOOKS, INC.
P.O. BOX 249
VALLEY FALLS, NY 12185

FIRST EDITION: MAY 2017

CREDITS
EDITOR: STACIA SEAMAN
PRODUCTION DESIGN: STACIA SEAMAN
COVER DESIGN BY MELODY POND

WICKED FRAT BOY WAYS

PHIL I stopped listening to him a couple of minutes ago. It doesn't matter. He just wants someone to listen to him drivel on and on.

He won't notice, either, that all I do is smile and nod, my eyes as wide open as I can make them without worrying about them popping out, and all I am saying is "oh" or "really" with the right, interested inflection when I can tell by his tone that some noise from me is required for him to keep talking. He's probably the most conceited and self-absorbed alumnus I've met, and that is saying something, since I've never met any alumnus who isn't a boring drone who stays involved with the house because they think it was the best time of their life, and being active in the alumni association somehow makes them still a part of the brotherhood.

I prefer the ones who just write a check when they get a fundraising letter and never come around.

I mean, I get it. When you're putting in sixty hours a week at some high-stress job and then coming home to a bunch of spoiled kids and a trophy wife who spends all your money faster than you can make it and your own mortality is staring you in the eye, you miss your days in college living at the Beta Kappa house when you didn't have an asshole boss and your phone wasn't blowing up all the time with needy asshole clients who act like you're their own personal slave and all you had to do was show up for class and study every once in a while and you spent most of the rest of your time drinking and smoking pot and snorting coke and fucking every girl you could get so wasted she couldn't say no or stop you from taking their clothes off and doing what you wanted. How many times have I had to listen to some alumnus whose body has gone to seed, who's gone bald, and whose best days are long behind him relive the debaucheries of his youth, getting that sad faraway look in his eyes as he thinks back fondly to that time before he had to be at the office all day only to come home to some bitch of a wife and deal with assholes all the fucking time, remembering when they didn't have to deal with all the horseshit they have to put up with to get the damned paycheck to keep up the front that they're living the American fucking dream?

It's pathetic, really.

It's just another reason I am glad I am gay.

Take Rubin Monterro, for example. He's the classic example of the Beta Kappa alumnus. He's got a glass of the expensive Scotch I keep in the president's office for when the rich bastards come by to play big shot and make me grovel for donation money. Rubin is not just any alumnus, he's president of the damned alumni association for our chapter, and he's driven all the way up here to San Felice from Beverly Hills for something. He usually comes up once a month to check on things, hang out, drink some Scotch, and ogle some of the Little Sisters or sorority girls—he especially likes to drive up during Little Sister Rush week.

His monthly visit—and I do consider it to be the same fucking thing as a period—was just last week, so I wasn't expecting him today. He caught me off guard when he called this morning and said he was heading up for a visit. I've been waiting now for twenty minutes for him to get to the point. He wants something, something is up—I don't know which, but it's fucking irritating as hell that he won't just get to the goddamned point.

My cheeks are starting to ache from the phony smile.

It's ironic, though—calling him was on my to-do list for today. Well, he was about four numbers down on the list of people I was going to call, but since he's here I might as well ask him first. He always makes me sweat for the money. He always writes the check, but he likes to make me feel like a whore before he does.

That's why he's the last one I will call out of the five I can always count on for an emergency donation.

This time will be different because he wants something from me, from the house. This isn't a social call.

I just have to wait for him to get to the point.

He will eventually, if I should live so long.

And when I know what he wants—I'll ask for the money.

It's all part of the game the chapter president has to play: Suck Up to the Alumni.

It's a small price to pay for the perks of being president.

I let my mind wander a bit as he keeps talking, gesturing, the Scotch swirling around inside the glass. I notice the bottle of Scotch sitting on my desk is about half-empty, so I make a mental note to give Joe Altamura a call. He's an alumnus, too, and owns a string of liquor stores up and down the California coast, from Eureka down to San Diego. San Felice has two of them, one near the campus and the other up in the hills where the rich people live. Joe always gives us kegs at cost and will donate cases of the good stuff we need to keep on hand for when some alumnus like Rubin comes by that I'll have to schmooze and suck up to and work for a donation.

Joe gets it. He was president when he was an undergraduate. He remembers what dicks alumni can be.

Even though they know the chapter isn't swimming in cash at the best of times, we can't give any of our distinguished and respected alumni cheap booze before asking them for money.

I never ask Joe for money. Free liquor and cheap kegs are more than enough.

Sometimes he'll send us a check without being asked. He gets it.

Rubin doesn't get it. He was never chapter president. It's not hard to guess why, either.

He was probably a douchebag then, too.

Let me make a game out of this. So, what's the over/under for him getting to the damned point?

I look at him. At least another five minutes.

Rubin Monterro is a big-deal entertainment lawyer. At least, he thinks he is. And like every lawyer I've ever met, he loves an audience. He knows, as chapter president, I have to listen to the alumni association president as long as he wants me to, which makes me loathe him even more. Now he's dropping names of his big important clients. Every time he drops a name I look appropriately impressed and say "wow" and "cool" when he stops to breathe.

I fucking hate playing games. But that's what I signed up for when I ran for president.

And I am good at playing games.

That's how I got elected in the first fucking place.

Middle-class boys from Santa Rosa don't get elected president of Gamma Rho chapter of Beta Kappa fraternity at the University of California–San Felice without being good at playing games.

"You have such an interesting life, Brother Rubin," I say in my sincerest voice when he takes a drink. "All those celebrities!"

"They're just people, Phil," he says with a wink. "Neurotic, crazy people with a lot of talent and money, but still—people."

I laugh, because he wants me to.

He holds his glass out, and I splash some more Scotch into it.

I know more about Rubin Monterro than his current wife probably does—and for the record, she is the second

Mrs. Monterro, former Heather Brady, *Playboy* centerfold and aspiring starlet who appeared in slasher movies and was usually killed after showing her enormous, not-enhanced-by-a-surgeon breasts. The first Mrs. Monterro's name was Lisabeth. She has custody of their two children and lives in Malibu. She came from money, of course, helped Rubin get a leg up in the business.

The divorce was her idea. She now has a live-in lesbian lover who still works as a tennis pro.

Rubin's parents were immigrants from Mexico who scrimped and saved for him to go to college. He was a scholarship student here and had to work all the way through college. I've never quite figured out how he wound up as a brother of Beta Kappa. It may have been a diversity thing—when I look at the chapter composites from when he was a brother here, he was the only Hispanic face and there was a black brother, too. He went from here to Stanford Law and used his fraternity connections to get a job with a big entertainment law firm. He made partner in five years and is now the managing partner.

And he's president of the alumni association.

I look at him and wonder what it was like for him when he was a brother here, working when all his lily-white spoiled rich-boy brothers had trust funds and credit cards and never had to worry about where the next six-pack was coming from.

I sometimes wonder if that's why he's such a dick as a president of the alumni, if he's somehow trying to get even with the brothers who treated him like the help when he was an undergrad.

I've done my homework on him, but he hasn't done his on me.

I know that he has three brothers and two sisters, all of them blue collar. I know he helps them out financially but they aren't welcome at his home in the Hollywood Hills—there aren't family holiday parties there, and his kids don't mix with their cousins. All of those nieces and nephews are blue collar, too.

I wish I could just tell him that I'm not some spoiled rich kid, too.

But that's not the game we're playing.

He wouldn't appreciate me knowing about his background any more than he'd respect me for mine.

If anything, he'd hate me for it, make my life a living hell.

And I need him to write us a check for a new air-conditioning system because the current one was installed back during the Reagan years when Rubin was an undergraduate and it's starting to go on the blink, and the hot Latino guy who came by to check on it on Monday said it was on its last legs and could go at any moment and it's fucking July in San Felice.

The a/c guy was hot.

I definitely need to get laid tonight.

I tune Rubin back in just in time for some more name-dropping about who he had lunch with last week and who he's going to see at the party he's going to at "George's"—I guess I'm supposed to assume he means Clooney and make the appropriate awed noise, because name-dropping assholes like Rubin Monterro always assume that everyone is as awed by A-list celebrity names.

It's all I can do not to yawn. I don't give a rat's ass about celebrities.

Unless they're writing me a check, I don't want to hear it.

I just want him to get to the point so I can ask him to write the check and send him back on his merry way to LA.

The sooner the better. I glance over at the clock. Joey will be back from the pool in about twenty minutes.

His dick is always hard when he's finished with practice.

There's no bigger crime than wasting a big hard dick.

I don't like to commit crimes.

Rubin is *still* talking.

"Come on, come on," I say to myself.

We do have the money to pay for the new air-conditioning system, but the house's cash flow is always hit and miss during the summer, and I'd rather get an alumnus to write a check to pay for it. There's barely enough money in the checking account to pay for the kegs for the Baby Bash party next week. If I ask Dr. Strickland to authorize a cash transfer from our reserves to pay for the air-conditioning system, he'll make me cancel the party. And he sure as hell won't transfer money from the reserve fund to pay for a party.

Asshole. I glance at Rubin. I wonder if Rubin feels about Dr. Strickland the way I do? Maybe we could get him replaced as comptroller...

Which means sucking up to Rubin even harder.

The party has to happen. It's a tradition. We've been throwing it for over thirty years.

Canceling the party is not how I want to start my presidency.

Get to the point, get to the point, get to the point.

He needs something from me—if he would just get to the fucking point already.

As he keeps blathering on, I wonder what he looks like naked.

He looks good now, but he was stunning in the composites, even with college-boy acne and bad 80s hair. He's wearing a tailored suit and he doesn't have a paunch, but I've never seen him in jeans or a T-shirt. His shoulders are pretty broad and his waist isn't small, but his shoulders are definitely wider. He's a Hollywood player, though, so he probably goes to a trainer three times a week and gets a weekly massage and probably plays cutthroat tennis on the weekends. I bet he took lessons for years, too—he didn't learn how to play tennis in the barrio. He's smart, always has been smart, and did what he had to do to reinvent himself.

You'd never know now he came from nothing just by looking at him.

You got to respect that.

Even if he is an asshole.

I glance down at his legs. The pants are tight in the legs, and the legs are pretty thick and hard. His shirt hugs nice pecs. He shouldn't wear his hair slicked back the way he does, though—it makes him look like a gangster, like he's Mafia or something. Maybe that's the look he's going for, something from *The Godfather* or *Goodfellas* or one of those other old movies people his age get hard over, spaghetti operas. He's still handsome, too. Not quite the looker he was when he was in college—I bet the girls used to drop their pants for him all the time.

He probably still gets a lot of action.

He's shifting uncomfortably and takes another big drink.

Here it comes, at long last.

Finally.

I give him my undivided attention.

"And so my nephew is transferring here," he says. He mops sweat off his forehead.

That's it? His *nephew*?

I scan my memory. He has several nieces and nephews. I wonder which one it is.

I try not to laugh, or even smile.

He drove all the way up from LA to tell me his nephew is enrolling here?

His nephew must be a total loser.

"And he's going to pledge Beta Kappa, of course," I reply smoothly, which I know is what he wants to hear. "He does want to pledge, doesn't he?"

Alumni are even more generous with their money when a relative is living in the house.

And Rubin is the only Monterro with money.

"Well, I want him to, but he's—he's not really sold on

the whole fraternity experience." Rubin Monterro looks uncomfortable now. "I've talked to him about it, of course."

I somehow manage to keep my face impassive, but I want to laugh in his face.

Oh, yeah, the nephew is *totally* some kind of dork or troll, a complete loser.

Rubin thinks we won't give him a bid even though he's a legacy, which pretty much makes the bid a formality.

"I'll send him a friend request on Facebook," I say, reaching for the bottle to pour more Scotch in his glass.

"He isn't on Facebook."

That stops me. I don't even know what to say to that. I steal a glance at Rubin. His forehead is wet with sweat now, even though I have the air conditioner on high.

We are sitting in the president's office, which has a window unit as well as the central air. Since the central air has been on the blink I turned on the window unit, and it's cold. I'm wearing a Beta Kappa T-shirt and a pair of jeans and am kind of wishing I'd put on a sweater. I wonder if I can go into my suite and get one.

"He's not?" I say finally.

"He—he isn't on social media."

Everyone is on social media. Something must be *seriously* wrong with him.

I resist the urge to ask if he eats paste. Instead, I put the cap back on the bottle and say noncommittally, "He isn't?" I smile. "Good for him. Social media can be such a time suck."

I'm making myself nauseous.

Rubin gives me a weird look and wipes his forehead again with his sleeve. "I know, I know, it's weird, I have kids, you know." He exhales and pulls out his cell phone. He fiddles with it for a moment, then turns it around so I can see the screen. "That's him. Ricky."

What the hell? He's fucking gorgeous.

I take the phone from him and look at it more closely.

Yes, he *is* model-gorgeous.

He's smiling in the picture, wearing a sleeveless dark blue soccer-style jersey with a gold stripe just below his pecs. His arms are muscular and defined, a thick vein running down from the shoulders along the biceps. His skin is dark, like Rubin's, but it glows in the sunlight. He has thick eyebrows and a strong nose, perfectly straight white teeth, thick lips, deep dimples carved into his cheeks, almond-shaped warm brown eyes. The soccer shirt is tight enough to show the ridges in his stomach.

He plays soccer, I think, unable to take my eyes off his face. That means he has amazing legs and a perfect ass.

Dear God.

So, what is wrong with him? It must be bad.

Rubin takes the phone away and tucks it back into his jacket pocket. "His name is Ricardo, we call him Ricky." He clears his throat again. "My brother..." He stops talking, makes a face, continues. "He married a girl from Mexico. She's very devout, very Catholic, goes to Mass every day. He is their youngest, they have two older kids, not very ambitious, no desire for college. He was the last one, you know, and it was a difficult birth...she had to have a hysterectomy after..."

Why is he telling me all this?

"And she got more religious, she shouldn't have ever gotten married, she wanted to be a nun but she fell in love with my brother, and Carmela, she well, well...she kind of pushed him to be a priest."

"A priest?" I raise my eyebrows politely, but it seriously is taking all my self-control to not burst into laughter.

He nods. "Like I said, Carmela...she's very religious. She practically lives at Mass, always saying her rosary...she wasn't much of a mother to those kids." He hesitates. This is a lot of personal shit he's dumping on me. He's probably wondering how much more he should tell me.

I am so getting that check out of him.

"She wanted one of her kids...she always wanted one of

the kids to go into the church, like that was some kind of extra credit or something she'd get in heaven." He rolls his eyes. "My mother was religious, but not crazy like Carmela. My mother thinks Carmela is crazy."

I mentally add another thousand to the check.

"Ricky was always a sweet kid, and my brother…my brother wasn't as involved with Ricky as he should have been." He scratches his head. "She always pushed Ricky toward the priesthood. And Ricky seemed to really, you know, want it."

"But not anymore?"

"He's been at Notre Dame the last two years, preparatory to entering the seminary." His face darkens. "He's smart, had some scholarships, but I was helping pay the rest for him, and Notre Dame isn't cheap."

"That's very generous of you, Brother Rubin."

He flushes even darker. "I'll keep paying for his schooling, of course, but now—now he's decided he doesn't want to be a priest anymore and he wants to come to school here—he'd already put in the transfer and got accepted before he told us." He looks grim. "On the one hand, I have to admire his determination." He twists the ring on his right hand. It's a Beta Kappa ring. I've never seen him wear it before. "But I think he should have talked to me about all this first."

Of course you do, since you're paying the bills.

"So, he doesn't want to be a priest anymore?" I find Ricky's dilemma mildly interesting. I've never met anyone with a deep religious faith, at least not to my knowledge. Then again, he was probably quite boring. "Lost his calling?"

Rubin is uncomfortable, which is a much more interesting twist to me than his nephew's supposed loss of faith. He shifts in the chair, takes another drink of the expensive Scotch, clears his throat, won't look me in the eye. Finally, he manages to say, so quietly I can barely make out the words, "He's gay."

You homophobic bastard.

"Beta Kappa takes our commitment to pledging standards

very seriously, Brother Rubin," I say in my most self-righteous voice. "And of course, the university's diversity commitment—"

"Oh, yes, your generation and all that PC bullshit." He waved his hand in a dismissive way.

Because *he's* not Latino.

He goes on, "I know we pay lip service to that idiocy, but you and me—we know how things really work, don't we? I don't want Ricky to getting blackballed because he's, you know, a *homosexual.*" He lowers his voice as he says the word, like he's ashamed.

Because, of course, he is ashamed his precious nephew is gay.

I bite my lower lip, trying to keep my own temper under control.

I want to tell dear Brother Rubin, president of the alumni association, that *I'm* actually a red-blooded get down on my knees so much I have callouses on them cocksucker.

I'm kind of surprised he *doesn't* know.

Which makes me wonder if any of the alumni know, or if they just pretend that the whole diversity movement of the university, all the progress we've made here at the house, is all just for show and something we wink at, pretend like we're complying and not really doing anything to comply?

But saying something to him now won't do any good.

We need that damned check from him.

It's pretty fucking galling.

Then again, did any of my predecessors ever report to the alumni that we actually have ten openly gay brothers in the house? There's bound to be some homophobia in the alumni association. Probably some racists, too.

We have a couple of Latino brothers, some Asians, an African American...

I glance over at the framed composite of last year's active brothers.

There's an awful lot of white faces.

If they didn't know about the gay brothers...it would be easy to look at that composite and think...

"I can assure you, Brother Rubin, that I will make sure that Ricky will be welcomed into the chapter with open arms," I say with a big smile on my face, making a mental note to make sure we actively recruit pledges of color during Fall Rush. "Does he know yet what he's going to major in?"

"Physical education." He couldn't sound more contemptuous if he said he was going to be a gardener. "He wants to be a soccer coach. He would have been a teacher at a Jesuit school had his *homosexuality...*"

It's amazing how uncomfortable he is just saying the word.

He takes another gulp of the Scotch. The glass is now empty, but I don't move to refill it again. "Ricky's a good boy, Phil. He's honest. He couldn't, in good conscience, serve the Church with the kind of desires he has...He was sinning in his heart, if not in his body, he said, and so he couldn't devote his life to God." He gets up and walks over to the air conditioner. He pats the top of the window unit. "I'm very glad to hear it, Phil. It means a lot to me that I can count on you to take care of Ricky."

You have no idea, Brother Rubin.

"Yes." I stand up. "Ricky is in very good hands here, Brother Rubin."

"I understand there's some issue with the air-conditioning system?"

I nod. "It needs to be replaced."

"It's a wonder it's lasted this long." He sits back down and takes his checkbook out of a pocket inside his jacket. "It was installed when I was a JA."

"Thank you, Brother Rubin."

"I'm counting on you, Phil."

"Ten thousand should cover it," I say. The quote was for

five thousand, but why shouldn't Brother Rubin pay for the party as well?

Homophobic asshole.

He tears off the check and places it on my desk. "I'd like for him to move into the house for the summer and live here during the pledge semester." He hesitates. "I want him to get the full benefit of the pledging experience, but…don't let the brothers be hard on him, okay? I can count on you?" He starts writing another check. "How much is the rent for the summer and the fall semester?"

I tell him and put both checks in the drawer where I keep the checkbook. "You can always count on me, Brother Rubin." We give each other the secret fraternity handshake, and I wish him a safe drive back to Los Angeles.

And once he shuts the door behind him, I smile.

I'll make sure we take *very* good care of your nephew, Brother Rubin.

And I know the perfect guy for the job.

BRANDON He runs out to the end of the springboard, muscles rippling beneath tanned skin, and bounces once on the end. He catapults up into the air, his muscles all tensed, his toes pointed, and presses his face to his knees and rotates several times at the peak of the leap. I watch, again amazed at the perfection the human body can attain, the beauty of the perfect lines he forms, his tight white bikini clinging to his hard, muscular ass like a second skin. His rotations complete, he straightens out into the air and knifes cleanly into the blue water of the pool with barely a splash.

"Bravo!" I call when his head pops up out of the water, his hair slicked back against his scalp, a broad smile on his face as he swims to the side of the pool.

It's the least I can do, since I'm not going to fuck him again.

No matter how much he begs.

And he will beg.

They always do.

I check him out again as he climbs out of the pool, water beading up on his skin and streaming down from his crotch as he shakes his head, sending drops flying as the wet curls unstick from his head and spring back like coils. He's handsome, no question about that—I'm sure the co-eds at Stanford can't drop their panties fast enough when he smiles at them. His skin is tanned very dark and the skin is smooth everywhere, no telltale hairs anywhere besides the ones poking out at the top of his almost obscenely low-cut bikini that doesn't hide the cleft between his ass cheeks in the back. Those dishwater blond curls that probably turn into ringlets, those long, deep, soulful almond-shaped green eyes…when he's finished diving, he should try to model.

The body is good enough for gay porn, but the dick leaves a lot to be desired.

The water in the pool might be cold, but it isn't *that* cold.

I slide my sunglasses back up my sweaty nose and reach for my poor margarita, melting in the afternoon heat. I take a sip. I have a bit of a buzz from the joint I smoked about half an hour earlier, and the tequila is keeping that edge going.

I'm in that almost perfect state of just buzzed enough to enjoy it.

And what is about to come.

He stands at the foot of my lounger, the tight Lycra hugging his package.

So beautiful.

Pity he's such a boring fuck.

He sits down on the edge of my lounger, dripping water onto my legs, and places one of his hands on my right calf, smiling at me. He's pretty, really pretty, but like so many other pretty "straight" boys, he's a boring fuck. He just missed the US national diving team at the trials a few months ago, and he's the diving star of Stanford. He's pretty boring about that, too. How many times have I heard about how he would have made the team if he hadn't blown the last dive?

I swear half the time I put my dick in his mouth to shut him up.

I've already fucked him a few times, but really, all he does is lie there and look pretty. Because that's all he's ever had to do. I'm sure all of his life pathetic girls have been so thrilled and honored to be with him that they are more than happy to suck his little dick until he shoots a load or fucks them.

I'd bet my next semester's tuition that Jaden Strauss has never given a woman an orgasm.

He wants me to fuck him.

He's got that look on his face, and his dick is getting hard.

Hard to hide that in a Speedo, even with a dick as little as that.

I'm a little buzzed, and a little horny, so why not?

His parents aren't home, and who cares if the housekeeper sees?

I take his hand and put it on my dick. "You want me, don't you?"

He licks his lower lip and nods.

"Go get the lube and a condom." I reach for the margarita. "And be naked when you come back out, lubed and ready to get fucked."

He bends over and kisses my dick through my bikini. I'm getting hard.

If only he could suck a dick worth a shit, I'd just let him blow me. It takes a lot less effort.

Little does he know this will be the last time.

"I'll be right back." He barely breathes the words out as he stands up, muscles rippling with every movement.

I knew he was a closet case when I met him. I only went to that party because I was bored. I'm still bored, really. Is there anything worse than the San Joaquin Valley in the summer? It must be a hundred and twenty degrees today. But visiting my aunt here in the international hotspot of Polk (that's sarcasm, if you're wondering) for a week or two is required by my mother, and it keeps the credit cards from getting cut off. She doesn't ask a lot from me—she's been a hands-off mother for as long as I can remember—and two weeks in this overheated hell is more than enough.

Even if I didn't need to get away from Jaden.

So I was invited to this party. My high school grades weren't good enough for the UC system, so I had to do penance for two years here at CSU–Polk. I joined Beta Kappa here and was so glad to get the hell out of here and head for San Felice I can't even begin to tell you. But I still know people here and got invited to go to this party in the Olive Grove part of town, where the old money of Polk—the ones who made money from raisins and the gold rush and the railroads built their houses and still lived well even as the money dried up—lived. That's where I saw Jaden, all five-eight of him, across the room in his muscle tank and shorts and dark tan. Someone told me he was a diver at Stanford and was engaged to his high school sweetheart.

I knew as soon as I saw him I could fuck him if I wanted to.

I was bored.

It really wasn't much of a challenge. The old joke about the difference between a straight guy and a gay guy being a six-pack is funny because it's true. A hard-on has no conscience, and straight boys want to get off. As long as no one else ever finds out, of course.

I fucked Jaden that night. At the party. In one of the spare bedrooms.

I think that was part of the thrill for him, you know? Knowing anyone could walk in at any moment, catch the straight boy with a big cock in his ass and loving every inch of it, begging for more.

And like so many other idiots who can't tell the difference between a good fucking and falling in love...

Yeah, leaving town would be the easiest way out.

He's entertaining enough for a couple of weeks, but love? Boring.

He'd probably go back in the closet. Not my concern.

I already have my plane ticket booked.

I wipe sweat off my forehead.

I watch his ass flex as he walks across to the sliding glass door, the muscles moving under the skin of his back. I've given him some good training—the next guy who fucks him will be in my debt. He really likes getting fucked, but he still has a long way to go before he gets a gold medal for fucking.

That makes me smile.

I'm pretty funny.

My phone vibrates and I pick it up. Phil's face is there on the screen, with that big cocky smile on his face, but impatient at the same time. He wants me to do something for him, that's what that facial expression means. He's up to something but he needs my help. He's smart about that kind of thing—you can't get elected president of the house without having someone to do your dirty work for you so your hands are clean.

If the brothers only knew. But they're idiots, for the most part.

Straight boys usually are.

I debate not answering it for a minute, and then figure what the hell and touch the Accept button. "What?" I ask.

"I got the money for the air-conditioning *and* for the Baby Bash party," he says. We're on FaceTime, so I can see he is in his bed in the presidential suite back at the house. A thin line of smoke is rising from the bowl in the bong on his nightstand. "You're at the pool? It must be hot as fuck there."

"Yeah, at Jaden's." His parents are both at work. Got to pay for that diving training. They think he's going to the Olympics. They're going to be disappointed.

"I thought you were done with him?" He smirks. "Don't tell me you feel something for him?"

"Hardly. Just one more time for old time's sake before I break it off."

"You're so generous. You give and give and give."

"After all, Beta Kappa is all about charity, right?" I take a sip from the margarita. It's melting, and the tequila's bite is almost lost in the watery taste. I reach for my baggie and start rolling another joint, putting the phone down between my legs so he can see my hard cock.

"Lovely view, bro."

"I thought you'd like it. It misses you, Phil."

Phil knows what to do with a cock. We had several memorable nights together when we first met, but soon realized we were too much alike. We've been friends and allies ever since.

Partners in crime.

But seriously, he's one of the best I've ever had.

He ignores it. I knew he would. He always does even though he knows I'm not serious. "You need to come back to San Felice as soon as possible."

"San Felice is only slightly less boring than Polk in the summer."

"But I need you here in San Felice, Brandon. I have a plan I need your help with." He licks his lips again and smiles. He really has the most terrifying smile.

Someone is going to get fucked over.

It is kind of tempting.

"So tell me." I smile back at him.

"I'd rather not tell you on the phone. You can be here by tonight."

"I'm coming back for the Baby Bash in a couple of weeks. Can't it wait till then?"

He sighs petulantly. "It could, but I don't want to wait that long. I mean…" He thinks for a minute. "I want it to be you."

"So why can't you do it yourself?" I ask as I lick the joint to seal the paper and reach for the lighter. I already know the answer. It can't be traced back to him because whatever it is, it's a shitty thing to do.

The president's hands must be clean.

Phil is just as big a whore as I am, but he's somehow managed to keep his reputation pure as the driven snow. The only reason the brothers even know he's gay is because he doesn't fuck girls. He's always been ambitious, always wanted to be president, so it's very important to him to have a good reputation around the house. Everyone likes him.

They don't know him the way I know him.

"Come back." His voice takes on a wheedling tone. "It's so boring here with you gone."

"It was your decision to spend the summer there, you have no one to blame but yourself. I told you San Felice is no place to spend the summer." I put the joint between my lips. "Besides, I'm not staying here much longer." I look at my watch. "I'm taking the red-eye to New York tonight at ten."

My aunt won't be sorry to see me go. She didn't want me to come, and we came to an understanding. She's not that much older than me—she's actually my mother's half sister. But my mother, as the oldest, controls the trusts my grandfather left behind for all of us, and my mother likes people to do what she wants them to. I don't know what bug crawled up my mother's ass to throw Aunt Lucy and me together for a couple of weeks—I think she likes to piss Lucy off because she's young, honestly. Meantime, my mother is off on a cruise with a bunch of her friends and my father is in Europe, I think, with his latest girlfriend, who's my sister's age. Maybe.

Lucy and I understand each other. I do my thing, she does hers, and no one's the wiser.

But I'd forgotten how fucking boring Polk was.

I've wasted over a week with Jaden Strauss.

"New York? What are you doing there?"

"I'm going to Fire Island. Jordy Valentine's rented a house for the summer." Jordy's father made more money than God inventing a computer program. Jordy pledged the Beta Kappa house at CSU–Polk before I transferred to San Felice. We fucked a couple of times—he has a big dick—but now he's all monogamy-minded with a hot architect whose name I can't ever remember.

Dante! That's his name. All muscle and olive-skinned with big blue-black bedroom eyes.

But they can't be that monogamy-minded if Jordy's spending the summer on Fire Island, on the other side of the country.

"If he's rented the place for the whole summer you can go anytime, you don't have to go tonight," Phil replies. "Come down to San Felice for at least a week before you go. You've got to meet this guy. I'll text you his picture." There's silence for a moment, and then my phone vibrates.

I touch the screen. "He's cute."

"Soccer player, wants to be a soccer coach."

Which means he has a great ass. And probably a great body. Soccer players always do. It's all that running.

"And get this—he was in training to be a priest but dropped out because he's gay."

"A virgin?" I yawn. "No thanks."

There has to be more to this, though. Phil wouldn't need me to seduce a virgin just because. I wait. He'll tell me soon enough.

"He's Rubin Monterro's nephew."

Ah, there it is. Phil hates Rubin Monterro. It's not just because he's alumni president. It goes deeper than that, but

I don't care. I don't care about Rubin Monterro, and I'm not interested. "I don't think so. Fire Island sounds better. Goodbye, Phil. I'll call you when I get there." I disconnect the call and put the phone back down on the table. I light the joint and take a deep toke.

He won't be happy, but he'll get over it. One of the things about our friendship is we know way too much about each other.

A virgin. That wouldn't even be a challenge.

Don't get me wrong, there's nothing wrong with virgins. I'm just not one of those guys who likes to break in new gays, you know? They almost always get too attached and make getting rid of them too hard. They cry. They stalk you. They keep hoping you'll change your mind.

Closeted guys are much easier to get rid of.

And seriously, if you've taught one guy anal hygiene, you've more than done your duty. Christ, teaching guys how to be good in bed is so tiring.

Some of them, though, are naturals.

A priest wannabe, though?

I'd have to walk him through every step of the way.

I ain't got time for that—just like I don't have the patience to do any more training of Jaden.

I hear the sliding glass door open and shut again. Jaden's walking toward me stark naked, his little dick hard and bouncing. He's got a condom and lube in one hand, another frosted margarita in the other one. I sigh. The margarita is welcome, of course, but his damned body is so perfect it's really a shame about the dick, you know?

Then again, that body will get him laid a lot.

You win some, you lose some.

It's a trade-off.

He puts the drink down on the table and pulls my bikini down. He gets down on his knees and takes me in his mouth.

"No teeth," I remind him as I take another hit off the joint.

I've been fucking him for over a week and I still have to remind him about his teeth.

He's lucky he's pretty.

At least he's good with his tongue.

He likes to lick my dick, which is good since he's so bad at sucking. He can't deep throat for shit, and his next fuck can teach him how to properly suck cock, you know? But he's good at worshipping. He likes having a dick in his mouth. I look over at my phone and pick it up again while Jaden licks and slurps and gets my cock nice and wet with his spit.

The guy is more than cute, really. He's pretty good looking—better looking than Jaden, and he's pretty.

I wonder for a minute why Phil wants me to fuck him—it doesn't really make sense. Why would Rubin care if his openly gay nephew was having sex?

But I forget about it because Jaden is putting the rubber on me and guiding me inside him, and he needs my full attention. I reach down and push him down on my dick while I shove up with my hips at the same time. His eyes open wide and he gulps for a minute.

"I've been too easy on you," I growl at him. "You want to get fucked like a little bitch, don't you?"

He nods, his eyes still bugging out. "Uh-huh," he manages to gulp out.

I shift my weight and get my legs down on the tile. I'm bigger than he is—he's maybe five-eight, one forty, and I'm six-three and about two twenty pounds of hard-trained gym muscle—so standing up with my dick still deep inside him isn't easy, but it's doable.

He's gasping and moaning as I get up. The movement is driving me deeper into him.

And he likes it. Oh, yeah, he likes it.

His eyes look into mine as I carry him over to the side of the house and lean him back against it. "Put your hands on my shoulders, bitch, and hang on."

I start pumping him, pulling out as far as I can with his legs wrapped around me and then trying to drive my cock not into him but through him as hard as I can. Every time he gulps and gasps and he's having trouble catching his breath and I just keep on, working a rhythm to match my heartbeat, out then in, out then in, and I can feel it starting inside me, and he is shooting cum all over my torso but I keep fucking him, fucking him deep and hard and he's trembling and gasping and drool is coming out of the side of his mouth and tears are running out of his eyes and he comes again and then finally I am, shuddering as I squirt my load into the condom. Sweat is running down my forehead as I slide out of him and lower him until his feet are on the ground. I keep holding him because he sways, like he can't stand by himself while his cum is running down my torso.

"Lean against the house," I say, letting go and walking over to get the hose. I wash his cum off me, pull the condom off, and neatly knot it, tossing it into the garbage can right outside the sliding glass doors. I rinse off my dick, turn off the water, and go back to the chair. I pick up my towel and wipe myself dry.

"Wow," he says, still leaning against the house, smiling at me. "That was amazing, Brandon."

"You're welcome." I slide my bikini back on, then my board shorts. I pull on my T-shirt and put my watch back on.

"You're leaving?" It finally dawns on him that I'm getting dressed. "But I thought—"

I slide my feet into my sandals and put the pinched-out joint into the baggie, which I toss into my gym bag. I put my sunglasses on.

He really isn't very smart.

"I'm going home, Jaden. I've got to pack."

"Pack?" He looks confused.

"You look so cute when you're confused," I reply.

"You're leaving?"

"Yup. Flying to New York tonight, heading out to Fire Island for about a week." I sling the gym bag strap over my shoulder.

"When—when are you coming back?"

I shake my head. "I'm probably not." I walk over and bend down and kiss him on the forehead. "It's been fun, Jaden."

"But I thought—"

I put my index finger over his lips. "Don't think, Jaden. It's not your strong suit."

Okay, that was a little mean.

"But—" He looks like he's going to cry.

"Don't cry, it's for the best." I kiss him on the nose this time. "Your girlfriend never has to know. And isn't that what you want?"

He starts sniveling. He is going to cry.

Time to get out of here.

"Good-bye, Jaden."

The gate swings shut behind me as I walk out to the car.

RICKY It breaks my heart to hear my mother cry.

My brother Sergio thinks I shouldn't have told her, but how could I go on living a lie?

It was making me crazy, making me unhappy. And God knows what is in our hearts, doesn't he? So I wasn't fooling God. How could I become a priest knowing what was in my heart, knowing that God knew what was in my heart?

I know what the Holy Father says, but I could not serve God with that on my conscience.

Father Romero, as always, was so kind and understanding. "You're having a crisis of faith," he said to me when I confessed everything to him at long last. "The feelings aren't a sin, the act is a sin. Yes, you sin in your heart when you think those lustful thoughts, but maybe it's best for you to go out in the world. If your calling is true, you will find your way back to God."

If only he had been the one to tell my mother.

Her parish priest is not so understanding. Father Juan refused me the sacraments.

I hope I won't have that problem in San Felice.

Father Juan wasn't the one who found—no, I can't think about that now. It wasn't my fault. Father Romero said so, no one blamed me for it.

And of course I couldn't tell Mama about it.

"Don't be stupid, Sergio, hard as it is," says my oldest sister, Lupe, who's twenty-five, as she lights a cigarette. She puts down the window of the old Buick she is driving so the smoke can go out the window. "It doesn't matter why he left the priesthood. Mama had her heart set on one of us going into the church, you know that as well as I do." She grins at me over the headrest.

"I think maybe if he had told her before—"

"She would have told him to stay at seminary." Lupe sucks on her cigarette. "And Father Juan can go fuck himself. Sorry, Ricky."

I smile back at her. "Say ten Hail Marys."

We all three laugh.

She goes on, "But it was sneaky, Ricky. Transferring schools and everything without telling anyone until it was a done deal."

"No one could talk me out of it once it was done," I reply.

I'm not proud of doing that. But it's true. I know myself better than that—I am very self-aware.

I knew I was gay when I was a little boy, and I also knew it was a sin. I know that one of the reasons I was so eager to please—so determined to be a good boy, to study and get good grades—was because of the fear that people could tell.

It was why I played soccer, which I didn't like at first, but I knew if I was good at it people would like me. Playing soccer got me a scholarship to a good Catholic school—St. Anthony of Padua—and I thought, I thought and believed if I was a good Catholic boy, if I was able to make my mother happy, became a priest, joined the church, devoted my life to God and celibacy, everything would be okay and I would go to heaven.

But no matter how much I prayed, the feelings never went away.

I couldn't stop myself from looking at other boys in the locker room.

I couldn't stop looking at magazine ads with muscular male bodies.

I couldn't stop thinking about them, dreaming about them.

Prayer did not help.

No matter how many nights I prayed before sleep, I still dreamed about boys. I still dreamed about kissing boys and doing things to them that were against God. I still dreamed about what their skin felt like and how their lips tasted and how it felt to press their bodies up against mine. I dreamed about the guys in perfume ads and underwear commercials and sweaty athletes whose wet shirts clung to their bodies and professional wrestlers with their glistening muscles and the other boys on the soccer team with me, and sometimes I woke up in the middle in the night with my underwear wet and my— my cock hard and aching and my balls hurting with the urgent need and I would get a towel to wipe off my sheets and my body and change my underwear and pray again, pray to Jesus My Lord and Savior and Mary Queen of Heaven to forgive me, to take these horrible dreams and fantasies and sins and filth away from me.

Father Arturo would wrap my knuckles with a ruler when I would tell him about my torment, threaten me with purgatory and hell and Hail Marys and Our Fathers, eternal damnation unless I stopped, and I tried and tried but no matter how much I prayed about it, Mother Mary never answered me, Jesus never answered me, they just left me in torment.

I always felt so unclean, so dirty, so unworthy.

So I prayed.

And decided to enter the church. I couldn't give in to my sinful desires, ever, so a life of celibacy, praying for forgiveness, praying for the sinful thoughts to be taken from me...The only thing to do was dedicate myself to God and never give in to the lusts of the flesh, to never give in to desire.

It was hard but I managed. I managed to never put my hands on another man, to never give in to the need, the desire, that festered inside me.

"Are you going into the Church because you love God and want to serve him, or are you hiding from your desires?" Father Romero asked me when I finally confessed all to him, about the...the wanton desires that consumed me, the lusts, the Satanic desires. "That's not what being a priest means, my son. You can't hide from the world inside the Church."

He was the one who convinced me that I needed to go out into the world, to see if my calling was true.

I was afraid, so afraid. I am still afraid. I don't know what the future holds for me.

I don't know if I will be able to stand strong against sin. Against fornication.

So I didn't talk to either of my parents or Uncle Rubin because I know they could have talked me out of it so easily once I decided to face my sinful nature, to go out into the world and see if my calling was a true one.

My mother thinks it's only a crisis of faith, and cries, and thinks I'll go back.

For the first time in my life I refuse to give her what she wants to get her to stop crying.

I may go back. I don't know.

It's so hard to reconcile the truth of who I am with my faith!

Surely Jesus wouldn't want me to be so miserable, so unhappy, to live a lie?

How can love be a sin?

Father Romero helped me. He helped me apply for student loans to pay for UC–San Felice if Uncle Rubin was angry and refused to help me anymore. "It's a lot of money," he said, "but you want to teach, and there's a program that will get your loans forgiven after ten years of public service."

Father Romero helped me with the application process, the transfer, everything.

The only thing he didn't help me with was breaking it to my family.

"Be brave and remember the Lord is with you no matter what happens," he told me.

It wasn't easy.

I didn't tell my parents the gay thing. My mother would never understand that. Leaving the seminary was enough.

But I was honest with Uncle Rubin.

I told him the truth.

"I wish you would have talked to me before you did all of this," he said to me over lunch at some extremely expensive restaurant where I was very aware my clothes didn't fit in. "It took guts to take the risk you did—and you were right not to tell your mother about the"—he hesitated, wouldn't look me in the eyes—"gay thing. Where are you going to live in San Felice?"

"I applied for the dorms. I'm waiting to hear back. But the student loans will cover—"

"You're paying those back. My nephew isn't getting out of college owing those vultures his soul." He waved his hand. "You can join my fraternity. I'm the alumni president. I'll talk to the chapter president, get you a room there."

I wasn't so sure I wanted to join a fraternity, but Uncle Rubin was being so reasonable, so understanding, I didn't want to tell him that. I didn't want to disappoint him any further.

His words were understanding and kind, but I could actually see it in his eyes, the way he wouldn't look me in the eyes as we talked.

The shame. The disappointment.

I can only imagine how my parents will react.

He called me to let me know it was all arranged, my rent for the summer and fall was paid, and I could move into the house this weekend.

Which is why we are in the car driving north on the 1, boxes of my stuff in the trunk of Lupe's battered old car. She can afford a new one, but she is saving every penny she makes to pay for her wedding next summer. Uncle Rubin won't pay for her wedding. I know that bothers her. It's always bothered her and Sergio that rich Uncle Rubin always seems to favor me over them. They don't blame me for it, but I know it bothers him. He doesn't take her seriously, refuses to invest in her shop.

But he will pay for my college.

I know he wants me to be a lawyer like him.

I don't know what I want to do.

I was going to be a priest and a teacher.

But I don't have to decide now.

I don't think I want to be a lawyer.

I'm lucky with Sergio and Lupe. They love me and don't care about the gay thing. Sergio isn't sure I'm even gay because I'm still a virgin. He thinks if I have sex with a girl I'll change my mind. He doesn't understand how it works, but that's okay. I know he doesn't mean any harm by it. He will look me in the eye when he talks to me. I think if I fall in love he will understand and nothing will change.

"You need me to fix that knock under your hood before your engine goes bad," Sergio says with a wink at me. He works at a Buick dealership repairing cars. He knows everything you could want to know about cars. He's always fixed our cars for us.

"You can look at it when we get to Ricky's fraternity," she says, stressing the word *fraternity.* "So fancy, going from the seminary to a fraternity." She starts singing Ariana Grande's "Fancy" and blowing me kisses in the rearview mirror.

"It was Uncle Rubin's idea."

"Too good for the dorms." Sergio makes kissy noises at me, too, but I'm not going to let their teasing bother me today.

I'm not sure joining a fraternity is the right thing for me anyway, but I don't want to disappoint Uncle Rubin any more than I already have. I don't know anything about fraternities other than what I've seen in movies or on TV. We didn't have Greeks at Notre Dame, but sometimes fratboys came up from other schools for football games, and they always behaved badly. I mean, sure, we had kids at Notre Dame who drank too much and had wild parties like other schools, but the stories I'd heard from other students at Notre Dame—horror stories, really, about parties at IU and Purdue, stories about drugs and drinking and girls being drugged or gotten drunk and then assaulted when they were barely conscious—those were kind of terrifying, terrifying that kids could act like animals like that.

Lust is so powerful.

And to live in one of those places?

But I didn't have the heart to tell Uncle Rubin, after everything he's done for me and the way I kind of just threw it all back in his face. It may not be for me, but I'll get through it if that's what he wants. It's the least I can do, and it seems like it's really important to him.

Sergio is engaged to a nice girl who works at Lupe's salon doing hair, and they're also getting married in the spring at St. Aloysious, our parish church. Father Antonio will marry them but he refuses to speak to me. I've disappointed him. I was his star student, and my leaving the church and coming out as gay has disappointed him. He's refused me communion since I came home from Indiana, but as long as I am not acting on my feelings, I am not sinning. I will find a church in San Felice where the priest doesn't know anything about me and will get absolution there.

My faith is still strong. I say my rosary daily and pray to Our Father every day, and I find solace in my faith. The Lord is my father, and I find solace in the Holy Mother's love.

I close my eyes and lean my head against the window. It's two hours or so from Los Angeles on the 1 to San Felice. I say a prayer to Mother Mary about what's waiting there for me.

It may not be so bad.

PHIL He's even better looking in person, which is kind of hard to believe given how fucking hot he looked in the picture Rubin showed me.

I'm lying in the hammock slung between two palm trees in the house back yard, drinking an iced mocha and pinching off the end of the joint when a car pulls into the parking lot. It's hot, it's always hot in San Felice in July. It's hot as hell inside the house right now, but the air-conditioning is getting worked on so the brothers living in over the summer will stop fucking whining to me every day. Thank God.

It's not easy being polite and concerned all the time when some dumbass like Wes Preston, who doesn't lift a fucking finger around the house, is in your face bitching. Like I broke the a/c on purpose or something just to personally inconvenience *you*. But I just smile and let him know I'm getting it taken care of and just be patient a little longer.

Sorry it's too hot in your room for you to watch porn and beat off, asshole.

I make a mental note, though. I always make a mental note.

He may not pay for it right away. But he will eventually.

I am very patient.

Hate and wait is my motto.

It's amazing what you can get away with if you're patient.

I'm a little surprised Big Man Rubin didn't bring His Sainted Nephew down himself in his red Ferrari convertible. The beat-up old Buick with a cracked windshield and a big dent in the back fender says a lot about how Rubin really feels about his family, doesn't it? How much money did he spend on sending His Sainted Nephew to Notre Dame, and he lets his niece drive a piece of shit like that Buick?

Sainted Nephew clearly is the only relative that matters.

It must be killing Rubin that he's gay.

I make my face friendly and neutral.

I am going to be Ricky's friend. Take him under my wing and guide him through the difficult time of changing schools and pledging a fraternity.

Beta Kappa ain't no seminary.

I roll out of the hammock and straighten my tank top, drop my sunglasses down over my eyes, and walk out to where they are busy unloading boxes and suitcases out of the trunk of the car. The sister is pretty and has incredible nails, at least a half inch long with amazing designs on them. The brother is stocky, could stand to cut back on carbs and hit the gym, but not bad.

He'd do around two in the morning if nothing better was around.

But His Sainted Nephew is fucking gorgeous, even better up close. The hair is thick and parted in the middle in a hopelessly out-of-date style and long, almost down to the shoulders. It's bouncy and shiny and reflects bluish-black in the sun. His shoulders are broad in his faded navy blue Notre Dame T-shirt, which fits tight across the chest. The arms are thickly muscled. His waist is almost ridiculously tiny, the legs in his shorts thick and strong and covered with black hair.

And the ass.

Oh my God, the ass.

"Hi." I stick out my hand, hoping I don't reek too much of pot smoke. "I'm Phil Connors, president of Beta Kappa. You must be Ricky Monterro. Your uncle said you were on your way. Welcome."

He smiles and I catch my breath. The dimples are deep, the chin strong, the eyes light up. His teeth are perfect and pearly white.

I'm tempted to fuck him myself. But that can't happen.

No matter how tempting it is, I have to keep my hands off him.

My hands must stay clean.

I can't believe Brandon is being so difficult about this.

I'm doing him a favor.

Maybe if I send him a shirtless picture...

"Yes, I'm Ricky." He shakes my hand vigorously. His hand is dry and bigger than mine and strong. "It's nice to meet you." He looks deep into my eyes and I almost drop to my knees right then and there.

No, I must stay strong, but I definitely need to get laid tonight.

"This is my sister Lupe and my brother Sergio," Ricky says as Lupe shuts the trunk. She picks up a box and smiles at him.

"You going to take good care of our little brother?"

I flash the smile that opens the bank accounts of the alumni. I shake hands with Sergio and pick up a box before I say, "I'm going to do my best. Follow me."

I've put Ricky in a room on the first floor on the side of the house facing the Sigma Pi parking lot rather than the backyard. Brothers are going to bitch about him being on the first floor anyway when they come back and get their room assignments in the fall, but it's standard that summer live-ins get priority.

I can also say, "His uncle got the a/c fixed. Cough up a check and I'll put you on the first floor."

His room is conveniently just down the hall from my suite. The hall is dark and smells slightly of stale beer and pot smoke. I see him make a funny face at the smell. Nothing I can do about that, so I just smile.

It's hot as hell in the hallway and I start sweating, and I can see sweat run down the side of his face. I apologize again about the air-conditioning. I unlock the door to room 7 and stand aside. Every room comes with two single beds, two desks, two chests. The small closet is divided in half. Brothers who get their own rooms can refurnish if they prefer, and we store the furniture in the attic. The room smells a little stale and it's warm. "Sorry again it's so damned hot," I say, leaning against the door frame. "They're still working on replacing the a/c. They should be done soon and the house will cool down."

"This is...nice," Ricky says uncertainly.

"If you want a mini-fridge for your room, just let me know," I say as he turns around and pulls out bedding from a box. He bends over the bed to put on the fitted sheet, and that ass...

My God, that ass.

I shake my head. "Anyway, my room is down the end of the hall—the one with *president* on the door. That's the office. Just ring the bell. If you knock and I'm not in the office, I may not hear you, so always ring the bell."

He straightens back up and smiles at me again. "I'll do that." He nods at me.

"If you need anything...it was nice meeting you both."

They nod back at me and I head back to my suite, wiping sweat from my forehead.

It's deliciously cool in the office.

He's so nice. So sexy.

I have a full bathroom, complete with shower, in my suite, but that doesn't mean I can't use the communal shower on the first floor.

My God, that ass.

I can't believe he's Rubin's nephew.

I can't touch him.

But that doesn't mean I can't help him get a little more experienced, does it?

There are plenty of guys who'd like to get a hold of that ass.

But I have to be careful, can't be too obvious, can't do anything to piss off Rubin. He can't know I'm behind it all. That would be too obvious, for one thing, and for another, it's so much more fun to be an innocent party when Rubin goes fucking nuts about his nephew turning into the biggest sloppy ho at Beta Kappa.

Got to get him past that religious thing, though.

Stupid fucking Brandon would be perfect.

I pull out my cell phone and start to text him, but drop my phone back in my pocket.

No, I'm on my own until he decides to come back to San Felice.

I hope he's having erectile dysfunction problems on Fire Island.

Bastard.

BRANDON I kind of like Fire Island. I can't believe I've never been here before.

New Yorkers, of course, think this is hot.

They couldn't handle San Felice in the summertime, that's for sure.

Sure, it's warm, but the breeze from the ocean makes a big difference. San Felice also gets a cold wind off the ocean, but it's sure as hell not over a hundred degrees here.

Glad I came.

The house Jordy's renting has five bedrooms and a pool, and a boardwalk down to the beach. Right now we're the only two here—I just missed his boyfriend and some of their friends, and some more people are coming in tomorrow. But for today it's just me and Jordy. It's kind of nice, not having spent any time with Jordy in a while.

Jordy's a good guy, always has been. I've liked him ever since he first pledged the chapter at CSU–Polk when I was there. He's inside right now, making a pitcher of Pimm's Cups. He's already been here for a couple of weeks and looks great. He's always tanned easily because he has olive skin, and the body! That body is bangin'. When I first met him when he pledged, he was kind of doughy and soft. But he hired a trainer and a nutritionist and turned himself into an underwear model. He's not quite as ripped now as he sometimes is—he says he's not been watching his diet as much as he should—but it's not noticeable unless you've seen him before.

I wonder if he and Dante have an open relationship? Or if they'll do three-ways now? Is Dante a top, or do they take turns? Dante's ass—that would be a waste if he didn't bottom. Jordy's got a pretty hot ass, too. He's also got a really big dick.

Jordy is one of the few guys I've let fuck me.

I'd let him fuck me right now.

And I'd love to get in between him and Dante one night.

That would be almost like doing porn.

He hands me a glass. "So glad you decided to come, Brandon. How long do you think you'll stay?"

I take a sip and it's perfect. "A week, maybe. Longer. As long as you can stand to have me here. It's kind of nice here."

"Glad you like it." He smiles. He's wearing a black bikini and sits down on the lounger on the other side of the table from me. A gull squawks and flies overhead. It's very peaceful there. Jordy opens a cigar box and pulls out a joint and a cigarette lighter. He sparks it and takes an inhale, passes it to me. "Dante is sorry he missed you," he says as he exhales. "He won't be able to come back out for another couple of weeks." His face twists.

"I'm sorry I missed him, too," I say. Jordy always has the

best pot. Then again, he can afford it. Must be nice to be sitting on a trust fund you could buy Haiti with.

But it's not like he's cheap or anything. Most guys with that kind of money are arrogant dicks. Jordy's cool.

"Why are you staying out here all by yourself all summer?" I decide to address it head-on. "Is everything okay with you and Dante?" I pass the joint back to him, feeling pleasantly high already.

He laughs. "Everything's fine. He's supposed to be here all summer, too, but a job that should have been finished last month isn't quite over yet." He frowns. "This should be the last two weeks. He's hoping to be done sooner."

"Are you still going to Oxford this fall?"

He nods. "That's going to be hard enough—so yeah, this is disappointing." Jordy is wicked smart. I never really quite understood why he went to CSU–Polk instead of Harvard. He had the grades, he had the money, he had the brains. He always says he wanted to go someplace "normal," whatever the hell that's supposed to mean.

I think there's more to the story than that. No one chooses Polk if they have another choice.

I only went there to get my grades up so I could get into San Felice.

"And—since I know it's on your mind, yes, Dante and I are talking about having an open relationship." He winks at me.

He knows me too well. It's a good thing we don't go to the same school anymore.

"But not until I go to England. Celibacy is too much to expect when we're on different continents." He hands the joint back to me. "And I'm not going to dump Dante for getting off with someone while I'm over there, you know? I love him too much for that, I'm not throwing away our relationship because he got horny. That's crazy."

"And vice versa, of course." I wink at him.

"I'm not looking for anything to happen, but…" He shrugs, the veins in his shoulder muscles bulging out as he does. "I also don't want to lose Dante if I do something stupid."

"A hard cock has no conscience!" we say in unison, and laugh. We clink our glasses together and drink.

"Someone's arriving tomorrow, and I want you to be on your best behavior." Jordy gives me his stern look. "I'm deadly serious, hands off on this one."

I wave my hand tiredly. "I'm bored with boys, Jordy. I think I'm going to swear off fucking for the rest of the summer." I take another hit off the joint and lie back on the lounger, closing my eyes. I feel perfect, that moment when you're high and buzzed from alcohol but not drunk or so high you can't function. The sun on my skin, the cry of the gulls, the waves, is all so relaxing I don't feel like getting off the lounger ever again.

"So you say now," Jordy says. "Wait till we go out for happy hour later. Lots of hot men on the island, my friend. But I'm glad to hear it. I don't want you touching him or getting any ideas about him."

"I'm not even curious," I say, but I am intrigued now. "But I am curious why you're so worried."

He laughs. "His name is Dylan Parrish, and he's transferring to San Felice this fall, as a matter of fact, and he's a Beta Kappa from UCLA." He explains the roundabout way he knows Dylan, but I don't pay much attention. I love Jordy, but he always goes into too much detail when he's explaining. It's part of that genius thing, I think. Beta Kappas are all connected somehow—someone always knows someone who knows someone who knows someone. Dylan apparently knows Blair Blanchard, who graduated from our chapter right before I pledged and now is working on Broadway. His parents are movie stars, and Dylan's mother apparently is an actress and was in a movie with Blair's dad which is how somehow Jordy knows him. Blair and his partner lived across the hall in the apartment complex Jordy lived in before he moved in with Dante.

That's the gist of what he is saying, anyway.

"I told you I am going to be celibate for the rest of the summer," I reply when he gives me a chance to finally say something. I wave my hand without opening my eyes. "Dylan could be a Calvin Klein underwear model. Wouldn't matter."

"I don't believe you."

"You'll see."

"It doesn't matter anyway," he says casually. I glance over at him. He's refilling his glass with ice from the cooler and more Pimm's Cup. "You wouldn't get anywhere with him even if you weren't celibate, Brother Brandon."

"So it's a moot point." Of course now he has me interested, damn him. I wasn't interested—stupid Jaden is still texting me, and so is his stupid girlfriend, wanting to know why he broke up with her, and I've already decided the next time she does I'm texting back *because he likes to suck cock you stupid bitch* because I don't owe him anything, so why shouldn't I blow off his closet door? And so I'm not really up for anything besides some no-strings fun, and that certainly doesn't include fucking some kid who's going to be living in the same house as me when school starts again, but why is Jordy so sure I wouldn't have a chance with this guy?

"It is. He's engaged."

I can't help it. I start to laugh.

"He *is* engaged, you heartless cynic! He's in love."

"That's so nice."

Jordy cuts me a look, so I don't say anything else. He'll start talking in a moment anyway. Jordy is also a believer in true love and romance and happily ever after. Why wouldn't he be? He has a gorgeous lover who's crazy about him, and they've been together for over two years now and they'll probably spend the rest of their lives together and wind up being one of those old couples who dress alike and spend every minute together and get written up on those tiresome gay websites as examples of True Love for the rest of us sad, lonely queens, proof positive that if we are all patient enough and good enough and hold out for the real thing, someday our prince will come.

You know, all that tired bullshit they start force-feeding little girls when they're in their cribs.

Jordy thinks I'm cynical about love, but I've never been in love. I'm sure the condition exists, but I'm not an emotional person. I never have been. When I was little I didn't dream about the man I was going to marry when I grew up. I always knew I was gay. I always knew I wanted to suck dick. I started when I was in junior high school. Straight boys don't care who sucks their dick as long as someone does, and I was a jock, besides. Jocks can't be fags, you know, even in the public school I went to, and I never had a girlfriend but no one ever gave me shit about it because I was big and strong and I had all the jocks behind me.

I was sixteen when I got a fake ID and went to my first gay bar. I met a hot older guy there that night and I went home with him, and he would have probably shit all over himself had he known how old I really was but instead he was so fucking excited to have me there in his house and naked in front of him and he sucked me for a while and then he wanted me inside him and I couldn't believe how nice it felt to be inside him, how good it felt to be fucking his tight ass, and I could also watch myself in the mirror on the wall behind the headboard, and don't believe those stories about boys shooting immediately because I certainly didn't, I was a natural at fucking and I loved fucking him and I loved how much he was loving being fucked by me and I fucked him twice before he drove me home and gave me his number and asked me to call him because he wanted me to fuck him again.

I wonder what his name was?

Damn, I'm getting horny just thinking about it, so I flip

over onto my stomach so Jordy can't see my erection and think I'm getting turned on talking about this Dylan kid.

"Dylan," Jordy says finally, "wrote an essay for Out.com about commitment, monogamy, and marriage." He's fidgeting with his phone and he hands it over to me. "See?"

I lift my sunglasses and peer at the screen. The headline screams at me A LIFETIME COMMITMENT, which makes me want to laugh out loud. There's a picture, too, two decent-looking guys beaming at the camera. One is in a dress Marine uniform, complete with the hat. They look way too young to be getting married and way too young to be that happy.

I bet they won't look so happy when they're getting divorced.

I wave the phone away. "They're cute."

"They met when Dylan was a sophomore in high school and Marc was a senior. Marc went into the Marines—that was his dream, and once Dylan got into college they got engaged. Dylan dreams of being a journalist—"

"A dead profession, poor boy."

"And so of course *Out* jumped all over the idea of him writing for them, he may even do a love advice column—"

I make a gagging noise.

"And this piece has gotten hundreds of thousands of hits. He's kind of become a bit of a celebrity this summer."

"Good for him! Has he started a YouTube channel yet? How many followers on Twitter?"

"I always forget what a bitch you can be," he observes. He relights the joint, which has gone out. "But when he arrives, you can suggest a YouTube channel for him. You are going to be nice to him?"

"Why wouldn't I be?" I smile at Jordy. "I won't touch him, and I'll be nice. Are you happy?"

Although...the poster boy for gay marriage and monogamy?

There's a challenge.
One worthy of me.
Maybe I'll extend my stay on Fire Island...

KENNY I'm in love.
I don't know what to do.
I've never felt like this before.
What do I do?
His name is Ricky Monterro and he's just moved into the house. Phil brought him by my room to see if I could help him out, since he's new and going to be pledging and I'm a junior active.
He's so beautiful.
I mean, there are lots of good-looking guys in the house, and some of them are even gay, and some of them I've heard will do things with you even though they're not gay if they can blame it on being high or being drunk but I've never tried I can't believe this beautiful angel dropped into my lap like this oh God what am I going to do someone who looks like Ricky would never look at me twice or give me the time of day or anything and I don't know what I am going to do I can't stop thinking about him he's so good looking and his body is so amazing oh my God oh my God oh my God and he's just downstairs from me and he's so good looking and he's nice too and I don't know what to do maybe I should talk to Phil he's always been so nice to me.

PHIL Maybe I don't need Brandon here after all.

RICKY My first night in Beta Kappa house and my first date.
My first kiss.

I am lying here in my bed staring at the ceiling and I can't sleep. I can't sleep because I am so excited. Coming here was the right thing to do. I made the right decision!

It's almost like a sign from God…

I wish there was someone I could talk to about this, share my excitement with. I've never been aware how lonely I've been. I don't have any friends that I can text or call. I don't feel comfortable enough with Sergio or Lupe to call them. I mean, I know they love me and they don't judge me…but details about dating a guy?

I think about it all again. He knocked on my door right after Sergio and Lupe had left me and I was finishing setting up my room. The knock was so soft that I wasn't sure I'd actually heard it, and I thought maybe Sergio or Lupe had forgotten something, or maybe it was Phil, seeing how I was settling in? He's so nice, too, and so good looking. He made me feel so welcome.

Anyway, there was a knock on my door, and as I wondered if I'd imagined it there was another knock, so I walked over to the door and he was standing there, all red in the face and embarrassed looking, and like he didn't know what to say to me or what to do. I said hello and he stuck out his hand and said, "Hi, my name is Kenny, and Phil asked me to kind of watch out for you since you're new here and I was just a pledge last semester."

I invited him in and he sat down in my desk chair. "Where are you from?" he asked, still stammering a bit. It was really cute, he was really cute.

So I told him about being from LA and going to Notre Dame before deciding to come here, and I asked him why he joined Beta Kappa.

"I wanted to join a fraternity because I wanted some place to belong." He was turning even redder with every word. "My high school…I'm from San Bernadino…was pretty homophobic. I got picked on and bullied a lot. I was in the choir, I like to sing."

"Oh, that's terrific! I sing, too. I was in the choir at my school and it wasn't that bad." It took me a minute to realize what he'd said. "Your high school was homophobic?"

"I came out when I was a freshman. I mean, everyone was already calling me a fag, so I figured how bad could it be, and then I got to college and even though the university has a non-discrimination policy...I wanted to join a fraternity but some of them say they aren't homophobic but they don't have any gay brothers but Beta Kappa does, I mean we even have a gay president now." He said it all in a rush like he was afraid if he didn't get it all out he wouldn't have the courage to say it at all.

"So you're gay?" I asked, just to be sure.

He was now so red he was almost purple. I mean, I've read that in books but I've never seen anyone actually turn purple in real life. He just nodded and he wouldn't look me in the eyes.

"I'm gay, too," I replied. "I haven't really gotten used to saying it. I'm gay. I'm gay. That's why I left Notre Dame. I was in the seminary. I couldn't stay there. Besides, it's so cold in the winter! I missed California winters."

"You're gay?" He looked like he didn't believe me.

"I'm gay," I replied. "Have you ever had a boyfriend?"

He shook his head. "I've had some crushes but I've never had a boyfriend and I've never been with anyone and so I'm still a virgin." His face was starting to go back to its normal color. "What about you?"

"Me, either. I mean, I just came out. My parents don't know. My uncle knows, though. I didn't know Phil was gay."

"I know, right? You'd never know. Sometimes I wonder if gaydar is just a myth."

"Gaydar?"

He giggled. "We're supposed to have this sense so we can tell if someone is gay or not."

"Well, mine must not work."

We talked for a long time, and then we were hungry so we walked to the Togo's a couple of blocks away and he bought me dinner (my first date! I can't believe it!) and we talked a lot more, and then we decided to walk down to the beach and walk along there, and it was already getting late and the sun was setting in the west over the water and we just talked so much, about everything, about music and what we liked, and we sang a couple of songs together and we were able to harmonize almost perfectly together without even trying—

Like we were meant to be, kind of.

And then we came back here and he gave me a kiss and I thought about asking him and making out with him but then thought that might be kind of slutty and so I said good night and here I am, lying in bed thinking about him.

My phone chimes.

He texted me.

Thanks for a beautiful night.

Coming here was so the right thing to do.

Totally.

BRANDON "There's a difference between attraction and love," Dylan is saying, very self-righteously, as he grinds pepper onto his salad.

He arrived about an hour ago; Jordy went down to the dock to meet him. I'm hungover and a little sore from last night. Jordy and I got good and baked and went dancing at the Pavilion last night. I drank a lot of beer and danced a lot and met some muscleboy from Chelsea with abs I could grab with my fingers and an ass that needed to be on my face and razor stubble on his pecs and ingrown hairs on his balls. We sucked each other and then I brought him back here and fucked him until he came a couple of times and I finally shot my load all over him and then I went to sleep hoping he'd be gone when I woke up, and he was.

My dick is sore and I'm getting a zit on my balls and my head feels like it's going to explode.

"And there's no rule that says you have to have sex with everyone you find attractive," Dylan says, offering me the pepper mill. "It's so...I don't know, 1970s to just drop trou for everyone who winks at you."

"1970s?" Jordy raises an eyebrow and looks over at me. He isn't hungover in the least, the asshole. He never gets hangovers. I don't know how he does it. "I mean, yeah, I get it. The sexual revolution, gay rights, everything had its start in the 1970s. But I don't understand the equivalency, you know?" He's managed to put together the most amazing lunch, an enormous bowl of salad with everything you can think of in it, including shredded turkey and avocadoes and onions and watermelon, with club sandwiches on the side, in quarters with the crusts cut off, skewered perfectly by toothpicks. "And besides, Dylan—you shouldn't judge people whose morality is different than your own."

"I don't judge people for their morality."

"Sounds like it to me." I pick up my glass of LaCroix grapefruit and wish it had vodka in it. I suppose this preachy little bitch doesn't drink, either. "What does it matter to you if other guys are horny and want to get off?"

He gives me a patronizing little smile. He's cute, I'll give him that. He's maybe five foot six and a natural blond, one of those who are so blond that his eyelids are pink, but he's also one of the lucky ones whose hair turns white in the sun and skin turns reddish gold. His eyes are a startling bright yet pale blue, big and round with long curly white lashes above and below. One of his front teeth is crooked and there's some gaps between his lower teeth. I wonder why his parents didn't get him braces. He has a sturdy little body, strong thick legs and a bubble butt and a flat stomach and a dewy freshness to his skin, which looks like it would be soft and silky to the touch. His legs are covered in thick white-blond hair, but his chest is smooth. One really pink nipple keeps peeking out from the side of his tank top. "Life is about choices, Brad," he says. His voice is even more condescending than the look he is giving me. I can see one of Jordy's eyebrows going up in amusement. "And people are their choices, don't you think?"

"Maybe." I shrug my shoulders a little bit. "But most people make choices on the spur of the moment and don't think them all the way through. If you did, you'd spend most of your life trying to make up your mind. I don't believe you should judge people for spontaneity, Dave. And my name is Brandon, not Brad."

He colors a little bit. "Sorry, Brandon. Mine's Dylan, not Dave."

I smile back at him. "I know."

He looks me right in the eyes. His eyes really are pretty. "Have you ever been in love, Brandon?" He emphasizes my name, and I can see a bit of a twinkle in his eyes.

If I didn't know better I'd think he was flirting with me.

"I've not, sad to say." I sip my LaCroix. "But I don't feel like I'm missing anything. You'd say it's because I don't know what I'm missing, right?"

"I like being in love, don't you, Jordy?"

"I do," Jordy says, wiping some mayonnaise off his face with a paper napkin. "But I also didn't know what I was missing before I met Dante and fell in love with him." He gets a faraway look in his big brown eyes. "I thought I was in love before…"

"When did you know you were in love with Dante?" I change the subject. I don't want to talk about Chad and I'm pretty sure Jordy doesn't either. "Before or after you had sex the first time?"

"Sex and love are different things," Dylan says before

Jordy has a chance to answer, but Jordy does give me a grateful look.

Chad is still a sore subject for both of us.

Probably always will be.

Besides, he has nothing to do with what we're talking about.

"I was drawn to him when we first met," Jordy says, and too late I remember that Dante was dating Chad when we all first met him. Jordy winks at me. "It's okay, Brandon, I appreciate it but I can talk about it. And it kind of fits into the conversation anyway."

Dylan looks back and forth between us, confused.

"Brandon and I met, Dylan, when I pledged Beta Kappa at CSUP," he goes on. "Brandon was only there so he could get his grades up to transfer to San Felice, but he was pledge brothers with a guy named Chad. I was different when I pledged...I was fat."

"Out of shape," I amend. "You were never fat, Jordy."

"Thanks, but that's how I felt. Long story short, I fell for Chad. I thought I was in love with him and he felt the same way, but I was wrong. I was crushed when he told me how he really felt, that I repulsed him."

That's not exactly how it went down, but it's Jordy's story to tell, not mine. It kind of sucked because Chad was my friend, too.

"I got in shape and I wanted to get even with him," Jordy was saying. "He did date Dante for a little while—that's how Dante and I met—but they broke up and Dante asked me out. I was attracted to Dante but I was trying to get even with Chad. That's why I went out with him at first, to get back at Chad. We fell in love." Jordy bites his lower lip. "I'm not proud of it, but I was insecure back then. Dante made me feel like I deserved to be loved, you know? He made me feel worthy. I'd never had that before...so it was easy for me to fall in love with him."

"And the sex was good, right?" I say.

Jordy laughs. "The sex is fantastic."

"So, let me ask you, Dylan." I turn my aching head to face him. I do feel somewhat better—the food is helping—but my head still aches and I long for a joint. "Have you ever had sex with anyone besides your fiancé?"

"No," he replies.

"Then how do you know you're in love with him and it's not just passion?"

"Because I miss him, and not just physically," Dylan says. "I feel better when he's around, you know? And I'm worried about him every second. I mean, he's in the Middle East, doing a tour in Afghanistan, and I won't even get to see him again for months. He could be killed"—his voice starts to shake here, his eyes getting wet, and for a brief moment I feel sorry for him before I get mad at myself for feeling sorry for the judgmental little prick—"before we get married. I may never see him again. And that goes a lot deeper than missing the sex."

"But you do miss the sex?" I ask, finishing the last of my sandwich. The headache is starting to go away too, and my eyes don't hurt anymore.

"Of course I miss the sex! Don't you miss it, Jordy, when Dante's back in California?"

Jordy clears our empty plates and carries them to the sink before answering. He brings back another can of LaCroix for me and another small bottle of Pellegrino for Dylan and sets them down before he starts rolling a joint. "I do miss Dante. I miss sleeping in his arms, I miss the feel of him in the bed with me at night, I miss having a warm body next to mine," he says, not looking up from what he's doing, "and I do miss the sex. I miss laughing with him and seeing his smile and being able to know he loves me just by looking at him. When I look at him sometimes I feel complete. I know that sounds sappy, Brandon, sorry, but it's true, that's how I feel. But it's different. We're only separated for weeks at a time now, and then he's going to be here for the rest of the summer. But when I'm at Oxford…" He licks the joint and lights it, taking a big drag. He waits, smiling at us as he holds the smoke in before expelling it and coughing. "I may need physical satisfaction. Jacking off can only hold you so far. I will probably give in to it sometime. Dante probably will, too. But I love him, and he loves me. So it won't be the end of the world. It's about separation, not about not loving each other anymore."

"I disagree." Dylan takes the joint from him and takes a hit.

Because of course you do, you arrogant shit, I think.

I take the joint from him as he says, "If you really love someone, you won't have sex with someone else. You can't."

"You mean *you* can't." I take a hit and feel so much better. I should have gotten stoned when I woke up. "But you don't speak for everyone else. You can't."

He looks me right in the eyes. "Okay, you're right. But I am not going to have sex with anyone other than Marc, and Marc will only have sex with me. For the rest of our lives."

And in that moment, I know I am going to fuck him.

I am going to fuck him, and he is going to like it.

He's going to beg me to fuck him and his heterosexist bullshit.

"That's so nice," I say aloud. "I really do envy you, Dylan."

PHIL If there's anything more sickening than watching two virgins fall for each other I don't know what it would be.

Kenny is such a timid little mouse I'm surprised he even had the nerve to take up my suggestion that he mentor Ricky. Ricky at least has the religious excuse, you know? But Kenny?

I would have fucked Ricky senseless that very night.

But Kenny is perfect for this. Ricky's religious mania will preclude him from just being seduced or having a one-night stand. I could tell when I met him he's one of those pitiful "I have to be in love" queens. Kenny's one of them, too.

I wish I could somehow figure out how to record them the first time they do it. It would be a laugh, fumbling around with each other and not knowing where anything goes or how to do anything and probably shooting their loads early without any penetration. Neither one of them would have the slightest idea how to give head.

Damn you, Brandon.

But Ricky might have been able to resist letting Brandon teach him the ins and outs of fucking, probably say a Hail Mary or something and cross himself. Falling in love with Kenny, though? That's perfect. And my hands are clean.

Once he and Kenny have done it, though, then we can work on getting him truly corrupted.

I'm sure Brandon will be interested once that happens.

Ricky doesn't know how lucky he is.

I'm still grateful to the man who taught me how to suck cock, how to get fucked, how to fuck someone properly. We all need a teacher, right? It's not like anyone is born knowing how to have sex the right way. The ancient Greeks had it right: pair up an older guy with a younger one so he can be mentored and learned.

I'll always be grateful to Coach Mueller.

He was my wrestling coach in high school, and I wanted him almost from the moment I first laid eyes on him.

I wasn't the first kid he seduced, and probably not the last, either. But I never for one moment assumed he was in love with me—even though he kept telling me he was—because he had a wife and kids and I wasn't stupid. What kind of life was possible for Coach and me? He wasn't going to leave his wife to live with a fourteen-year-old. I just wanted to get off, and learn how to get other guys off, and I needed someone to practice with. Watching porn online wasn't enough. Sure, it helped when my dick was hard and my balls ached and I needed relief, and watching it helped me understand some things, but I needed practice on a real human.

I looked young for my age, so going to a gay bar or meeting someone online wasn't going to work. I didn't want to find some pedophile online and then have my body be found weeks later in the woods.

No, I needed a man with a lot to lose and someone I had easy access to.

Coach Mueller fit the bill.

I didn't go out for wrestling because of Coach Mueller. I went out for wrestling because I wanted to be able to touch other boys' bodies without getting gay-bashed or called a fag or anything. I liked that it was an individual sport, too. I hate that whole team mentality bullshit I had to put up with in Little League. Fuck that shit. And everyone got boners during practice, so it wasn't like me getting one was a big deal. It was just part of the sport, no one thought anything about it as long as you didn't blow your load in your singlet.

I worried a couple of times I was going to, but so much concentration is needed, and you need to focus every part of your body, so getting off isn't exactly something that's going to really happen anyway. The two times it almost happened for me were when I was practicing with Darnell White, a senior, whose skin felt like velvet and his body was amazing and his ass was so tight and round and hard and I was so attracted to him I would have sucked his huge dick in the shower in front of everyone if he'd let me.

I still dream about how big his dick was.

My guess is Ricky is one of those guys who go from virgin to whore in five minutes. Once he gets off he's going to be insatiable.

And he's in the right place for it. The nice thing about fraternities is even the straight boys will do shit as long as they have the "I was drunk, I don't remember" cop-out opportunity later.

Kenny, though. Christ, he always looks like a scared rabbit. He's wandering around all the time with this dreamy look on his face and a half-smile—whenever he isn't spending every waking moment with Ricky.

How do I know they haven't fucked? I asked Kenny, who tells me everything. There's no such thing as oversharing with him. I smile and listen.

Kenny...like I said, timid. He's living in a fraternity house with at least ten other openly gay guys and he's still not popped his cherry yet. Because he's afraid to approach anyone. Because he's afraid someone will say no. He's told me so. I have even considered fucking him and getting it over with, but it's been kind of fun watching him. He tries so hard not to look at other guys in the showers. Nobody cares. Go ahead and look, dude, but he's so afraid someone is going to punch him in the mouth or something for sneaking a peak.

Um, even the straight boys look, dumbass.

He's a cute guy, but man am I glad I didn't go to whatever homophobic hellhole his high school must have been to scare him off sex so much. I spotted him when he went through rush, stammering and blushing and scared to death. I was rush chairman with my eye on the prize—presidency—in the election at the end of that semester. He was nervous and scared and shy, and I knew why. I knew why he was rushing Beta Kappa.

Scared little gay boy.

So I singled him out for attention, talked to him, talked to everyone, introduced him to everybody, got him to bid. I wasn't his big brother—I told him he was better off getting someone he didn't know as well, but I was still going to look out for him anyway—and I did. He was going to quit any number of times—the pledge semester is designed to make them want it by dangling it in front of them and then yanking it back away from them, threatening to drop them, making them want it so badly they could taste it by the end of the semester.

I knew it was all bullshit when I was a pledge but I played the game. I played it so well they didn't know—still don't know—that I think it's all a bunch of bullshit.

For me it's all about connections for after, not all this high-minded bullshit about brotherhood and helping each other out and community. Fraternities are like any other group of people. There's backstabbing and cliques and feuds and gossip and fights. I can't stand half of my "brothers," but they'd never know it.

The only person here I am even remotely close to is Brandon.

Anyway, Kenny came by my room to tell me all about Ricky and how he felt.

"I think he really likes me."

"Why wouldn't he? You're a great guy."

"But he's so handsome and sexy—"

"Don't run yourself down, Kenny. Believe in yourself."

Then I had to listen to all the details about their first date, how they walked over to Togo's and then down to the beach where they watched the sun set in the west and held hands and came back to the house and they kissed and Kenny wanted to ask him out again and did I think he would say yes and how fast should he go and on and on.

Christ, it's like listening to a junior high school girl talking about Zac Efron.

I suppose some people would think it cute, this whole Disney romance like he's Aladdin and Ricky's Jasmine going on a magic carpet ride and—I may throw up.

Someone rings my bell. I answer the door and it's Joey Henderson. Joey's almost six-six and has to duck to get through the door. He smells like chlorine and pot and sweat and hormones. His blue eyes are bloodshot and red from being in the pool and his huge dick is hard, I can see it through his shorts, which means there's nothing under the shorts except cock and there's razor stubble on his legs and broad chest and shoulders and he's here because he wants me to suck him off because all the testosterone and endorphins from swim practice have made his dick hard and even though he's high he wants to take a nap and he won't be able to unless he's gotten off and who else is going to blow him?

I close the door behind him and he drops his shorts off and lies back on my bed with his hands behind his head, his huge thick cock reaching up his torso past his navel and the trimmed bush around it over the pale strip of white skin where his Speedo rides low on his long torso, the muscular legs. He's tweaking and pulling on his nipples.

He likes that, he likes me to suck and bite on his nipples.

You're in for a surprise today, Joey, I think as I open the drawer on my nightstand and pull out two nipple clamps and snap them onto his erect nipples. His eyes open in surprise but then close to slits as he realizes how good it feels.

I get in between his legs and lick the underside of his cock. It tastes slightly like man musk and a bit of chlorine. He moans.

I kind of resent that he thinks all he has to do is knock on my door whenever his hard-on needs attention, but it's a nice cock. It's no wonder every girl he fucks turns into a stalker. I can't imagine what it would be like to have that monster inside me, and he's big and strong, too, with lots of endurance.

He'd probably put me through the damned headboard.

I start toying with his dick with my tongue, licking one side then the other, running it over the head, teasing the slit where I can taste a bit of precum. I cup his balls with one hand and wonder if I dare try to tease his prostate with the other hand? Sometimes he's fine with it and sometimes he's not, thinks it's faggy to have a finger inside his ass, which is hilarious because he thinks it's not faggy to have his dick in a fag's mouth, but he's not very smart to begin with. I don't know how he manages to not flunk out, he's really just a machine that swims and smokes pot and eats and fucks and studies some of the time, and I stop teasing it, I deep-throat him, which isn't easy and takes a lot of skill, but fortunately I am good at sucking cock, and I am working his dick with my mouth and teasing his taint by running my index finger from his balls to his asshole and then back again slowly, ever so slowly while holding on to his balls with my other hand and he's moaning, saying things like "oh yeah that's nice suck that big dick" because talking like you're in a porn movie is a turn-on, oh yeah, I can't even begin to tell you how big a turn-on that is for me, but my dick is hard too but I can't touch myself, I can't get naked with him because that would be faggy and I wonder again why I am doing this, what part of me kind of hates myself to put myself through this kind of abasement, debasing myself, and then I think about how many times I've recorded this with my laptop and how many times I've set my phone to auto take pictures, and know that ultimately I could destroy him if I wanted to.

That's why, of course, I remind myself.

He thinks he's using me, but I have power over him.

Power. It's all about power, isn't it?

I choose to suck him off.

And he does what I want him to do as far as the house is concerned, and he gets all his buddies to fall in line. I've never had to threaten him with anything, but if I ever need to I can. It wouldn't be hard to send the pictures and the videos to everyone on campus.

I own you, bitch, I think as he starts to stiffen because he's going to come and I can feel his balls starting to constrict as he gets ready and I pull my mouth and head back at just the right time as he shouts as he spurts all over himself.

I get up and go into the bathroom and get him a towel.

He wipes himself down and pulls his shorts back up.

"Thanks, brother," he says like he always does and leaves me.

I toss the cum towel in the laundry basket.

I need to get laid.

I need to get out of the house.

I pull out my phone and go to Grindr.

It doesn't take long, some junior who lives in an apartment close enough by for me to walk. I put some poppers and condoms and lube in my backpack and sling it over my shoulder. I brush my teeth to get the taste of Joey out of my mouth and walk a couple of blocks in the insane heat to the Alhambra Apartments. I knock on the right door, apartment 220-B.

The door opens.

Shorter than I would like, but he takes care of himself. All he's wearing is some board shorts. He has a Marvin the Martian tattoo on his right arm. He smiles at me. His hair is blond, buzzed short, and his dick is hard. He smiles and steps aside so I can go inside.

Once the door shuts he grabs me hard and shoves me up against the wall, shoves his tongue into my mouth while he strokes my dick through my shorts, and I cup his ass in both hands and he tastes vaguely like peppermint and I move my mouth down his neck and bite one of his nipples and he shudders, shoves his hands into his shorts and shoves them down and I slide one of my fingers between his hard ass cheeks, looking for the hole and then I find it, and smile to myself because he's already lubed and ready for me to get in there and I run my fingertip around the rim and he's already moaning and I tap the hole with my finger and his whole body flinches with every tap and he's breathing hard and he's undoing my shorts and I lean back, still tapping his hole with my finger and my shirt is coming up over my head and now he's licking my chest, toying with my nipples and he's breathing into my neck *I want you inside me* and we leave our clothes there and I put on a condom and he lies back on the carpeting in front of the television and I slide in between his legs and shove my cock inside him all the way and his eyes almost bug out of his head and his whole body is shaking as I stay there, straining and pushing to get deeper, I want my cock so deep inside him that it's in his throat and he's shaking and trembling and whimpering and I start sliding back out and his legs wrap around my waist like he doesn't want me to come out of him but I keep moving back until all that's left inside is the tip and then I ram down into him again, and he opens to me, and I start pumping, and his ass is amazing, it feels like silk and velvet inside, and I lean down and kiss him on the mouth, our tongues mingling inside as I can feel it, my own load rising inside, and he is pumping his own dick in his hand, and he shoots all over himself and I pound a couple more times and shudder and cry out as I come, it feels like gallons are blowing into the condom, and I am shaking and he is shaking and then we are both finished and I slide out of him and tie the condom off and he smiles at me and asks me if I need to shower and I say no I'm good and put my clothes back on and shut the door behind me and I walk back to the house, my dick and balls a little bit sore but I feel better.

I didn't even ask his name.

Probably better that way.

KENNY I feel like a pervert.

Ricky doesn't know it but whenever I can do it without him knowing it I take pictures of him. We went to the beach this afternoon to just hang out and get some sun and when he took off his shirt I almost died I mean he is so good looking and his body is just so perfect and I took pictures of him with my phone coming out of the water with his shorts clinging to every part of him and he's so good looking and oh my God when we got back to the house I downloaded them to my computer and I jacked off and now I feel so dirty and creepy and I don't know how I am going to face him again I feel so dirty I mean who does this?

RICKY Kenny is so wonderful, so nice, such a good guy.

I don't know if what I am feeling for him is love or not, but I smile whenever I think about him. I smile whenever I see him. All I want to do is spend time with him.

He is the sweetest guy.

Just this afternoon we went down to the beach. I feel so comfortable around him, and I've never felt that way about anyone before. I feel like I can tell him my secrets, I can tell him anything, and it won't matter. The walk down to the beach felt like I was floating on air.

I am so glad I came to San Felice. I feel so much more at peace with myself.

Last night I dreamed about Kenny. He's so cute, really, the way he smiles and his eyes light up and I like that he doesn't want to push me about…doing more than kissing. I want to, of course, I'm curious, and now that I don't have to worry about people judging me and…

…I still haven't found a church here in San Felice. I know there are several, but I don't know who to ask about which church might be more open to having me go there.

I don't want to be judged by a priest who will hate me and my sin.

But how can it be a sin? How?

God made me this way. I don't believe—the more I am away from it—that God could be so cruel as to give me these feelings as a test of my soul. I cannot believe that God would do this to me, would send me to hell for sinning.

We are all sinners. None of us are free from sin.

But how can love be a sin?

I don't like questioning my faith, I don't like questioning my teaching.

I don't like questioning God.

David and Jonathan loved each other, didn't they?

I know that the devil is a liar, that he is seductive, his tools are pleasure and passion and beauty. I don't understand. I don't understand anything anymore.

I still love God. I still love Jesus and the Holy Mother.

Why can't I love Kenny? Why do I have to choose?

BRANDON "You got in late last night," Dylan says to me over brunch.

"Keeping tabs on me?" I smile back at him.

"No." He starts to turn a bit red, which means he's lying. "I just happened to get up to go to the bathroom and I heard you come in around three. Where were you so late?"

We'd gone to a house party just down the beach, thrown by some theater people Jordy knows through Blair Blanchard, a bunch of singers and actors and dancers who were all amazing looking and had great bodies but boring as hell. All they wanted to do was gossip about other people they knew and name-drop people they've worked with, and after a couple of hours of that I was fed up and bored and needed to get the hell out of there, so I slipped out and went to the Meat Rack. There's an honesty about the Meat Rack that you don't get from phone apps or bars or parties, where you pretend to be interested in someone and you have to make conversation with them and act like you want to have a relationship and pretend that you care about them and have to listen to them drone on and on about the boring things that interest them so you can get their pants off and fuck them and it's hard to make a clean escape because they always want your phone number or some stupid promise to call or get together again when it was just sex.

Sometimes you just want sex.

And at the Meat Rack there's none of that stupid game

playing and dancing around, there's no talk or exchange of names or anything. It's about fucking and sucking and getting off and you don't have to go through the stupid shit. You'd think gay men would know by now that there's nothing wrong with having sex for the sake of having sex, and why do they always have to make something more out of it? Why do they lie to themselves and give in to the whole puritan bullshit about sex?

I got sucked off twice and I fucked two guys in the Meat Rack. Sue me.

"I got bored at the party."

"Where did you go?"

"Don't ask questions you don't want to know the answer to." Jordy is catching the ferry because he has business in the city for the day, but he'll be back tonight. He is rummaging through his shoulder bag, making sure he has everything he needs. "You two are going to play nice while I'm gone, aren't you? And don't forget, Blair and Jeff are arriving this afternoon. I'm going to try to make the same ferry, but if they get here before I do or I'm delayed—"

If I don't cut him off he will micromanage everything and we won't remember half of what he says. Jordy is a bit obsessive. "We're adults, Jordy. I know what room they're using and I'm sure they know how to use a kitchen or get food themselves."

"I was over-explaining again, wasn't I?" He gives me a weak smile.

"Go on already, you'll miss your ferry." I get up and shoo him out the front door. I turn back around and smile at Dylan. "Now we have the whole place to ourselves, what do you want to do?"

He looks nervous, like I'm going to rape him or something. I feel like telling him I don't need to rape anyone, but why not let him be nervous? "I think I may lay out by the pool and read."

I pick up the pitcher of mimosas and pour the last of it into my glass. "Do you want me to make some more?"

He frowns at me. "You drink a lot."

"And you're pretty judgmental. Do you ever have any fun?"

He turned redder. "I'm sorry if it comes across that way."

"It does." I smile back at him, batting my eyes. "You judge how much I drink, you judge my sex life—I'm surprised you don't judge me for going to the gym and working out."

"There's nothing wrong with keeping yourself in shape." He's turning even redder. "Jordy said there was a gym—"

"We can go over later if you want," I reply, yawning and stretching. I have my bikini on under my board shorts and I am not wearing a shirt. I know stretching makes my muscles flex and my abs tighten, and the shorts creep down a bit so the top of the bikini shows. He's looking, and when I catch him he looks away.

It's almost too easy, really. He could make more of an effort.

"Yeah, that would be great." He frowns. "I'm pretty confident, but some of those guys at the party last night—"

"They're professional dancers. Their bodies are their business." I shake my head. "Don't compare yourself to them. They take hours of classes per day to stay in shape and be ready to go onstage. Dance is incredible exercise, you know."

He smiles. "I hate doing cardio."

I smile back. "So do I, that's why I like to go dancing. Dancing is the best exercise."

"But you must live in the gym! Your body—" He cuts himself off.

It's all I can do not to smile. I decide to treat it as an innocent remark. "I work out a couple of times a week," I reply. "It's really about eating, making sure you're feeding your muscles and your body. We don't, as Americans, really look at food the right way, you know?"

He looks relieved. "No, we really don't."

"Of course, food should be about taste and flavor and satisfaction," I go on, trying to remember Jordy's trainer's words, "but we tend to think of food in terms of rewards—'oh, I did this so I get to have some ice cream,' that sort of thing. And it's okay to eat stuff that's not good for you every once in a while. If I crave something I just go ahead and have it. If I don't, I'll keep wanting it more and more and when I finally do give in—because I will—I'll binge on it rather than having a moderate amount. It's really about eating smart, you know?"

"I'd love to have arms like yours."

Seriously, this is going to be too easy. "Doesn't your fiancé have a great body? I mean, he's in the military, isn't he?"

He nods. "But he's more lean than big. I'd rather be bigger. I mean, I want to be lean but I want my muscles to be bigger."

"I'll be glad to help you get bigger, Dylan." I smile back at him. "Anything to make one of America's finest happy."

"That's…that's really nice of you." He hesitates. "I—I owe you an apology. I haven't been very nice to you."

I hold up my hands. "It's okay, really." I finish off the mimosa. "No harm, no foul."

"I just heard some things about you. I was warned."

"Warned?" I keep my voice calm, but inside I'm seething. Someone has been talking shit about me? I don't care what people think or say about me as a general rule—it's usually the truth, and you can't bitch about what's true—but if it's going to keep me from reaching my goal of fucking this kid, getting him to cheat on his fiancé, yeah, something has to be done about it. "Who warned you? What did they say?"

"A friend." He won't look me in the eyes. "When I told her I was coming here, she warned me about you. I'm not going to tell you her name, so don't ask me, but she did tell me about your reputation."

"And what reputation is that?"

"She told me that you'll fuck anything that moves and you don't have any feelings and you don't care who you hurt." He says it all in a rush, like he's been waiting to get it all off his chest and feels relieved now that he has, but he also looks sad.

"Wow" is all I say.

"I—I'm sorry."

"No, really, it's okay." I keep my face expressionless as I carry my plate and glass into the kitchen and rinse them off in the sink. He comes up behind me and puts his hands on the back of my arms.

"I'm sorry I told you. Are you okay?"

This is going well. "I don't want to know who said that about me." I could probably swoop in now, make him feel sorry for me with some sob story about my parents' many divorces and how I don't think my parents love me and how no one has ever understood me and so I try to get approval, get my self-worth, by using my body and see getting laid as valuation and make him feel so sorry for me he'd give in because no one would ever know because we are alone here in the house and who would believe me? No one would believe me no matter what my reputation is because he has his own reputation, and even though people are always so willing to believe the worst of other people, it would be my word against his and there would always be those who would doubt, who would think I was lying, trying to spoil something noble and pure.

No, I would need proof.

So, this is going to be a long game.

I'm going to have to be patient, but I am not only going to fuck this little bitch, I am going to break him and his precious Marine up, I am going to make sure that everyone knows he's nothing special. Fucking him isn't enough.

I am going to make him fall in love with me.

And I am going to break his heart.
And it's going to be fun.

PHIL I can't believe what I'm hearing.

I start laughing. I can't help it.

"Seducing Ricky Monterro wasn't enough of a challenge for you, but you're going to waste your time with Dylan Parrish?" I manage to get out while still laughing so hard that it almost hurts to breathe. "Oh, Brendan, just come home to San Felice and do me this little favor. I know Fire Island is fun, but what's the point of being there if you can't have any fun?"

"I didn't say I wasn't going to have any fun. I just have to be sneakier about it, is all." Brandon leers at his phone. "I'm pretty sure I can have a three-way with Blair and Jeff—they certainly were hinting about it last night."

"You and your couples." I wave my hand.

"Don't knock it until you've tried it. Are you still sucking off Joey?"

"It's starting to get boring for me." I didn't answer the door when Joey came by earlier. He can beat off for a while. I hate being taken for granted. And it's not like he can complain, either. Straight boys and Grindr hook-ups make life so much less complicated.

"How about Ricky Monterro? Amy progress there yet?"

"Oh, that." I'm starting to get a little impatient, and Kenny was most definitely the wrong choice. It's been days and they're still mooning around and haven't done anything besides kiss. I wouldn't believe them but they've both told me that—I've kind of become a father confessor figure to them both, but no matter how much I try to push them to finally get on with it, they both are adamant about taking it slow.

Like virginity is the ultimate prize or something.

But I have got to be patient, I can't be too obvious or rush anything. It's driving me crazy.

"Slowly but surely," I say. "You'd think they weren't young men. I should take them in for testosterone shots. I've never met two guys who were less interested in getting laid."

"Well, maybe when I come for the Baby Bash I can help push things along."

"So. You are coming?"

He nods. "Dylan and I just booked our flights."

"He's coming with you?" I raise my eyebrows. "Good work, Brandon. Are you going to try to get him drunk so you can take advantage of him?"

"I don't need to fly him to San Felice to do that," he says. "We're on Fire Island, remember?"

"So how are you getting laid without him knowing it? The Meat Rack?" I start to laugh. "Are you having to sneak out of the house so he doesn't know? Oh, Brandon, seriously, give this up and come to San Felice already. Ricky would be so worth your time, you have no idea."

He winks at me. "I can do this, I know I can."

"I'll bet you can't."

"You want to bet me?" He's amused, I can tell. "If I sleep with Dylan, what do I win?"

"A night with me." I laugh with him. "If you fuck him— and have proof—I'll be your sex slave for a night. But what do I win if you don't?"

"But I will win, Phil, you can be sure of that."

"But if you don't? What will you give up?"

"I won't have sex for the entire semester."

I roll my eyes. "You wouldn't be able to do that, either, and how would I ever know for sure? No, that's not good enough. Not if I'm putting up my body." I laugh at him, as he is seriously thinking about this. "What is my body worth?"

"Your body?" He leers at the screen. "I cannot tell you how many times I've thought about being with you again, Phil, the way we used to be, do you remember?"

This isn't funny anymore. I don't like to remember that.

"Well, I guess that's your motivation then, isn't it? But what do I win, if we're betting?"

"The pleasure of laughing at me? Knowing you won?"

I roll my eyes. "Yes, of course, Brandon, that would be a fair bet."

He smiles at the screen again. "Then it's done." He disconnects the call.

I put my computer to sleep and lie down on my bed.

Now that it's come up, I can't help but remember.

He transferred here two years ago, just after I finished my second year in the house and was already climbing the ladder to my end goal of being president. When we first met...I knew I wanted him. It's hard to describe, really, what Brandon is like. He's about six foot three inches tall, with a long torso and these deep-set blue eyes underneath a thick brow, a huge smile with a slight but sexy gap between his front teeth, dimples, tanned, and that body. My God, that body. He is lean and strong, with enormous biceps and thick pecs and a flat defined stomach and a gorgeous ass and the legs. Oh, the legs. He was a jock in high school and played football and basketball and baseball, and seriously, the smile is a game changer. The moment I saw him looking at me, I knew he wanted me, too. At that point in time I wasn't having sex with any of the brothers, it was a rule I'd come up with when I was a pledge. I knew that some of the brothers weren't completely comfortable with gay guys, so I thought if I kept it out of the house it would help me. I had decided when I pledged I was going to be president my last year, and I was working toward that goal.

But I was willing to make an exception for Brandon.

I didn't have my own room then, and neither did Brandon. We neither one of us had lived in long enough to merit our own rooms.

So, how to do it? How could we get together without anyone knowing?

He would send me text messages about what he wanted to

do to me and would send pictures of himself in bikinis, in his underwear, never really showing me everything but leaving very little to the imagination. My roommate that semester, Dan Rolke, had early morning classes and I would wake up after he left so I could lock the door and pull up the pictures Brandon had sent me on my computer, so I could sit there in my chair and lube myself up and imagine him on top of me, imagine what it would feel like to have his body on top of me, his lips on mine until I came. I've never wanted anyone so much in my life.

Finally Dan went home for one weekend and I had the room to myself, and I let Brandon know that this was his chance. He was also sleeping around a lot—I was well aware of what he was doing and who he was doing it with, and it's not like I was being celibate myself, but that Friday night after the house began to quiet down after the party—we always have parties on Friday nights—he knocked on my door around one in the morning and I let him in. He smelled a little of sour beer and pot smoke and he had some coke with him and we shut the door and I kissed him and led him over to the bed and he held some poppers under my nose and I was writhing as he took my shirt off and started working on my torso with his mouth and tongue and then he somehow had my pants off and he was sucking me and the blood was pounding in my head and then he was naked and we were lying together on the bed and he let me fuck him and it was amazing, no one's ass had ever felt like that before or since, and he worked with me as I fucked him and it was like we were having some kind of contest, a battle to see who would come first and I wasn't about to lose, no I wasn't, and I somehow managed to not come even though everything was aching and my balls were screaming for release, but I kept fucking him and then he came in an impressive eruption and I just kept fucking him, fucking him and trying to get all the way inside him, and I loved it all so much and then finally it happened and we cleaned each other up and curled up in each other's arms and went to sleep, and in the morning he fucked me, and that was how we spent the weekend, only getting dressed to go get food and shower and then come back to my room, and when the weekend was finally over my cock was sore and my balls ached and my ass felt like I had been reamed and he felt the same way and I told him the truth.

"We're never going to do this again."

"I didn't think so," he replied, kissing my neck. "We're too alike, aren't we?"

"I want to be president of the house, and that won't happen if I'm involved with a brother," I said to him, moaning a little bit as he worked his mouth down to one of my sore nipples, bitten and bruised so much that even the feeling of his breath aroused it, "and you're right, we're too much alike and we would only end up making each other unhappy. One of us would cheat and then it would get ugly." I touched his lips with my index finger. "I know we could have the kind of relationship where we could do as we pleased, but I don't think you'd be too happy knowing I was with someone else and I know I could never be happy knowing you were with someone else."

He nodded. "I couldn't bear to share you, no." He kissed the head of my dick. "So it's best if we just remain friends and allies?"

"Friends and allies."

I have wondered some nights, alone in my bed with my dick hard, remembering that weekend with Brandon, if we made the right decision, but I know in my heart we did. We would have only ended up hating each other if we tried to make anything more of it. There have been moments, of course, when I've seen him with someone where I have felt a pang in my heart, a wish that things could have somehow been different, but they couldn't have been.

We would have ended up hating each other.

Hard as this is, sometimes it is better.

It is better to be friends than enemies.

I lay my head back on the pillow and close my eyes. I slide my hand down under my briefs and start slowly stroking my dick. I push all thoughts of Brandon out of my head.

That wouldn't do. That wouldn't do at all.

Instead, I think about Joey's massive dick, how he tastes, the way I can utterly control him and dominate him with my mouth, how no one for the rest of his straight life will ever give him the kind of blow jobs that I gave him, for as long as he lives he will remember the pleasure I gave him...and at some point in his life he'll question whether he is actually straight or not.

That's what I think about as I jack off.

My power.

DYLAN Brandon is nothing like I thought he would be like.

He's a very sweet guy, with depths and feelings I would have never expected him to have based on what I'd been told about him. I was told he was selfish and shallow and uncaring, and none of that is true.

He's kind, and thoughtful, likes to laugh and have fun, and doesn't ever worry about tomorrow.

I...I kind of wish I was more like him. He's a nice guy.

It makes me wonder what my friend Joni has against him. When I told her I was transferring up to San Felice, she was adamant about staying away from Brandon Benson.

"There's a brother at the Beta Kappa house there you absolutely need to have nothing to do with," she said to me one day when we were out shopping. Her brother Kenny belonged to Beta Kappa there, and he'd told her stories about Brandon, stories she told me about while we looked for clothes for her trip to Europe. Joni and I went way back, to when we were kids and used to live next door to each other. We've always been the best of friends, but I never really got to know her brother Kenny very well. We both entered UCLA together—my parents wanted me to go to school locally before transferring up to San Felice—and I joined Beta Kappa and she was a Little Sister. She actually recommended Beta Kappa to me because Kenny was also joining Beta Kappa.

"Brandon Benson?" I asked when she came out of the dressing room, checking my iPhone emails. "What a weird coincidence. He's going to be staying with Jordy on Fire Island while I'm there."

"Cancel your trip," she said without missing a beat.

"I'd like to think I'm a better person than that," I said, a little insulted. She was my best friend and she didn't think I could honor my engagement to Marc.

He's off in Afghanistan risking his life and she thinks I'm going to hop into bed with some smooth-talking, entitled douchebag?

Thanks for the encouragement, Joni.

And she was wrong about him, anyway.

For one thing, I don't have to worry about being tempted because I'm in love with Marc. For another, he's not my type. I mean, he's a good-looking guy, there's no question about that. I can see why guys would be attracted to him. He has the most amazing blue eyes I've ever seen and they twinkle when he smiles; they look like they have stars in the blue. I almost wonder if they are real or contact lenses, I don't think I've ever seen someone with eyes like that before. But he's too tall for me and too muscular. I'm barely five-seven and weigh about one fifty, he's well over six foot three or so and he's got to weigh about two twenty. Marc is only a couple of inches taller than I am and he's a lot stronger than I am, but I'm never afraid of him.

Big guys make me uncomfortable.

Marc wasn't my first, even though I act like he was, but he's the only person I've ever told.

I was raped when I was fourteen.

My parents don't know, either. All they know is I got terribly depressed when I was a freshman in high school and they sent me to a shrink. I don't know why it happened to me. I blamed myself for a long time. I met a guy on the internet. He seemed like a nice guy, he was older, and we chatted for a long time. I mean, I always knew I was gay; I was never interested in girls that way—I only liked girls for friends, other little boys didn't interest me unless I thought they were cute or something, but I didn't really know any gay kids and so I found a chat room online for questioning teens even though I wasn't questioning, I just wanted someone to talk to about it and maybe find a boyfriend or something and I met this guy, his name was Allan, and he told me he was sixteen and went to private school. We talked a lot and soon we were texting each other and talking on the phone, and he seemed like a good guy and so he invited me over to his parents' house and I took the bus over there and when I got there he seemed older to me than sixteen, but he was also really big, about Brandon's size, really, but not nearly as good looking and certainly not as muscular, just a big guy, and when I wasn't comfortable with him kissing me, he forced himself on me and I tried to resist but he was too big and too strong and—

It took a while for Dr. Sablosky to earn my trust, but once I finally felt like I could tell him, that he wouldn't tell my parents, he worked on teaching me that what happened wasn't my fault and being trusting didn't mean I deserved to be raped.

Dr. Sablosky did want me to go to the police, but I wasn't about to do that.

It was bad enough for women, and too much time had passed.

My mother is a crime novelist, and she's always talking about how horribly women who get raped are treated by the system, so I can't imagine how they'd be about a gay boy.

Dr. Sablosky did a great job of convincing me that I was worthy of being loved and it was just a matter of time before I met a great guy and fell in love. He made me believe in myself again, and that was when I realized that this concept of gay promiscuity wasn't something I had to subscribe to just because I was gay; that the beauty of our society was that I could be gay however I wanted to be. I decided that I wanted to fall in love and I would only have sex with someone with whom I was in love. I wanted something like *The Princess Bride* or *Beauty and the Beast* or *Aladdin.*

I wrote about this a lot. I want to be a writer, like my mother, when I finish college, and I've always written. I wrote an editorial that got published on my school's website called "Someday My Prince Will Come" about holding out for being in love. It got a lot of hits and they asked me to start writing regularly for them. I'd never thought about being a journalist, but my mother told me if I was serious about being a writer I should do this, because it would train me to meet deadlines and to write even when I didn't feel like doing it.

My piece about monogamy was published in the UCLA *Bruin* originally, and that's when the editor at *Out* got in touch and asked me to rewrite it, add more to it and go into more detail, and they wanted to run a picture of me and Marc with it. I had no idea it would go viral the way it did, with people commenting on it and sharing it all over social media, and of course it pissed off some people.

I don't understand why everyone has to think that someone who has a different opinion than they do is criticizing them. I stopped reading the comments and started deleting emails unread.

I struck a nerve, apparently.

Even Marc, when we FaceTimed, mentioned that some of the guys over there had read it and thought I did a good job.

I miss him so much, and I worry about him all the time. We don't get much time to talk because of the time difference and what he's doing over there but...

"You look like you're going to cry," Brandon says. "Are you okay?"

We're walking to the gym to work out. He's offered to help me with my workouts, and it's so generous of him.

He's not what I expected at all.

Joni's not always right.

"I'd rather not say," I reply.

"Were you thinking about Marc?"

It's uncanny. That's the other thing about him. He always seems to know what I'm thinking. And he's so kind.

I nod. I don't know if I can speak without starting to cry right there on the boardwalk. I know it's silly but I can't help it and then he's putting his big strong arms around me and pulling me in close, and instead of feeling afraid and threatened I feel safe and loved, and I put my face against his bare chest and cry for a moment, and he's just holding me and stroking my back softly and I'm so mortified and embarrassed and when I try to pull away from him he doesn't resist me.

He wipes my tears away. "It's only natural to miss someone you love, Dylan," he says softly. "Are you okay now?"

I nod again. "Thank you," I somehow manage to say.

He smiles at me. "I so envy you. I've never been in love."

"Never?"

He shakes his head as we start walking again. "I haven't. I guess I've just not met the right person yet. Sometimes I wonder if I can love someone, or if I'm just unlovable."

"Don't say that. Everyone can fall in love, and you're not unlovable."

"I'm not?" He says it shyly, so softly that I almost don't

hear him over the sound of the gulls and the guys walking along and talking and laughing and the ocean waves. "You don't know me, Dylan."

"Maybe I haven't known you for very long, but I know you're very kind," I reply. "You're—you're nothing like I expected. I don't know what I expected, but you're nothing—I don't even know how to say this, but you're a nice guy, Brandon."

"There are a lot of people who would disagree with you about that."

"They don't know you very well."

He bows his head a bit. "I've done some things I'm not very proud of," he goes on as we walk into the gym. It's crowded, guys sweating and muscles rippling and weights clanking over the grunts and the sound of some dance song blaring over the sound system by Rihanna, I think, and we give our passes to the guy working the front desk and we head into the weight area. "I think we'll do chest and back today, does that work for you?"

"Sure." And he takes me through an exhausting workout, teaching me form and technique ("work out smarter rather than harder, Dylan") and we keep talking and he tells me about his loneliness, and how he actually doesn't really have a very high opinion of himself and he finds validation as a person in the attention he gets, his self-worth all comes from whether guys are attracted to him or not, and it's so sad it almost breaks my heart, and he tells me how every time he sleeps with yet another guy he feels emptier afterward, it always comes back to that.

"You slept with Jordy, didn't you? Before he and Dante got together?" I ask as we leave the gym, my heart breaking for him.

"Jordy and I were a lot alike," he replies. "That's what brought us together, I think, the loneliness and the lack of self-esteem. It never would have worked between us, but we did manage to stay friends. Usually the guys I sleep with don't want anything to do with me afterward." He shrugs those big shoulders, all veiny and defined and pumped now. "I don't really have a lot of friends."

"What about Phil Connors? Isn't he your friend?"

He scowls, wipes sweat from his forehead. I want nothing more than to get back to the house and jump into the pool and cool off. "Phil and I are friends, but not the kind of friends you'd think. You seem to know an awful lot about our chapter for someone who's never been there."

I laugh. "My best friend Joni's brother pledged last year. Kenny Gaylord?"

"Oh, yes, Kenny. Nice guy. I don't know him all that well—we don't hang out very much. You say his sister is your best friend?"

"We used to live next door to each other when we were kids." He is smiling now, looks very happy as I say this. "They moved away when we were about ten, but Joni and I have stayed friends. She's a Little Sister at UCLA chapter. Why are you smiling like that?"

"No reason. Just glad you're transferring to our chapter, is all. It'll be nice to have a friend in the house."

"You don't have any friends in the house?" This is so sad I can hardly stand it. At UCLA I consider all the brothers to be my friends. Some of them aren't as close to me as others, but I like all of them. They're good guys.

Maybe at San Felice they're different?

"Oh, we're all friends, I'm just—I don't feel close to any of them, is all. Like I said, I don't have a lot of friends."

"You have me now."

He pushes open the gate to the backyard. The pool surface is glittering in the sun. "You have no idea how much that means to me."

How could Joni have been so wrong about him? I think as I smile back at him.

I jump into the pool.

The water feels amazing.

KENNY My sister Joni is annoying.

You'd think my sister would show some interest in the fact I'm in love and met a great guy. She claims to be this big gay ally because her best friend is a gay guy and she's all about him and the gays and loves *RuPaul's Drag Race* and is proud to have an iPhone case that says FAG HAG on it and can't wait to be old enough to go to gay bars and gay everything, but she doesn't give two shits about her gay brother.

I don't know why I thought this would be different.

Joni's always thought I was an embarrassment to her.

When I was getting bullied in high school for being gay she never once stood up for me, never said anything to anyone, never defended me.

She'd fucking walk barefoot on broken glass for Dylan Parrish, though.

Joni can go fuck herself.

I'm tempted to tell her that but it's not like she ever gives me a chance to even say a word anyway.

No, I'm supposed to be excited that she's coming up for the Baby Bash, but she isn't coming to see me, she's coming to see Dylan. She fucking FaceTimed me from Europe to tell me this. It's bad enough Mom let her go to Europe by herself this summer with some of her friends.

I didn't get to go to Europe.

"It's going to be a surprise for Dylan, so don't tell him anything when you see him, okay?"

"I won't."

"And you can introduce us both to this guy you have a crush on."

I grit my teeth to keep from screaming at her. "We are dating, Joni."

"Of course you are. Just like you were dating Colby in high school, remember?"

I want to strangle her. "It's not the same thing."

Colby Whitfield was one of those stereotype golden boys you see in all the teen movies and TV shows. Star athlete and smart and nice and good looking and voted Most Likely to Succeed and all that bullshit. Colby was nice to me. Colby stopped people from picking on me whenever he was around.

Who wouldn't fall for Colby? Every girl in our school— my bitch sister included—was in love with him.

Colby was straight, of course. I was the only gay kid in our school, and even though I never came out, everyone knew I was gay. I've never been able to figure out how the nasty assholes do it—how they figure it out, but they have this mutant superpower that helps them figure out what everyone's weakness is. School was torture for me. I didn't have any friends. And my bitch sister was popular, and her best friend was a gay kid at another school and she enjoyed my misery. Every day I wanted to kill myself. Every. Single. Day. I thought about it every night before I went to bed and every morning when I woke up, and I thought about it at least two or three times a day. Online support groups were all I had, but I had to be careful and always make sure I erased my browser history because my bitch sister would rat me out to her bastard friends at school and they'd make my life even more miserable than they already did.

"Of course it's not," she says nastily, mocking.

"You'll meet him at the party," I reply, making a mental note to see how I can make Dylan's life miserable once he gets here. Oh, I can't wait to see her face.

I cut off the connection just as she starts talking again.

I hope she's not planning on sleeping in my room that weekend.

She can get a fucking hotel room.

I'm still angry about it when I run into Phil a few minutes later on my way to the soda machine.

"Kenny! Are you all right? You're shaking," he says, looking at me funny.

I shake my head. "I—I'll be fine."

"Do you want to talk?" he asks me. "You want a soda? I have some in my fridge in my room. Come on, let's go talk, okay?"

I follow him into his room. Phil has always been so nice to me. He's probably the nicest guy in the house. Before I know it I am crying and telling him all about my sister Joni and what a bitch she was to me and has always been and why is she so supportive to Dylan and so mean to me and Phil dries my tears and gives me a big hug and kisses the top of my head and tells me to just ignore her.

"Wait till she sees Ricky," he says, a big smile on his face. "And sees how much Ricky likes you."

"Thanks." I feel kind of stupid for crying in front of him, but she always does this to me. She doesn't even have to be around to humiliate me.

Why couldn't I have had a nice sister?

"And Dylan—her friend Dylan—he's transferring here this fall?" Phil is saying. "I thought I recognized the name. Transferring from the UCLA house, you said?"

"Dylan's not so bad," I lie. Dylan always treats me like I'm invisible. "He's engaged to a Marine serving in Afghanistan."

Phil smiles. "Isn't that nice?"

"Yes," I lie. I can't tell him the truth about how I feel about Dylan, Joni's precious Dylan, and his precious fiancé and—no, best to keep my mouth shut. I have Ricky, and that's more than enough. I don't want Phil to know how awful I am.

I don't want anyone to know.
I can't mess this thing up with Ricky.
I wouldn't want to live if I lost him.

PHIL Poor, stupid, naïve Kenny.

I'm tempted to tell him about Brandon's plans for Dylan, but why get his hopes up? Besides, it doesn't make me look particularly good to know about it.

Must keep up appearances.

Anyway, Brandon might not succeed. He doesn't always. And this Dylan sounds like a tough one. I'm looking forward to meeting him. The pictures I've seen of him online don't look like he's anything special. It must be the engagement that is so challenging for Brandon. I get it, I do; sometimes it gets boring playing the seduction game, especially when the other player is so easy. It's why I don't bother with any of the gay brothers in the house. They're all too easy. Look at Kenny, with his tearstained face, sitting on my bed upset because of his bitch of a sister!

Family. I've never understood why people are so hung up on their families.

I could go the rest of my life without seeing or talking to mine and it wouldn't bother me in the least.

"Stop giving your sister so much power," I say to him, and he turns an adoring face to me. Honestly, I could have the little fool right now if I wanted him.

Yes, I do understand Dylan's appeal for Brandon.

"She can only hurt you because you let her," I go on. "Why would you let her have that kind of power over you? She's your sister, but you don't like her. Let it go, Kenny, you'll be much happier."

I think of my own sister. I haven't spoken to her since I came to San Felice. I don't speak to my parents very often, for that matter. My mother always tries to guilt me into coming home for a visit and I just can't deal with them. Isn't Thanksgiving and Christmas enough? I send cards for their birthdays and call once a month like clockwork. What more do they want?

"I know it's hard," I say. "But trust me, you shouldn't give anyone that kind of power over you. Not even Ricky."

"But I love him." He looks confused. "Why would he hurt me?"

He's like a child. His parents—and sister—have really done a number on this poor kid's self-esteem. I mean, for God's sake, he is twenty years old and still a virgin. He's never had sex, he's never had a boyfriend, he's never been in love. It's no wonder he and Ricky haven't done anything yet.

They don't know how.

Maybe I can convince Brandon to help Ricky along a bit when he's here for the Baby Bash.

It's this coming weekend, actually, and I have the party completely planned. The kegs are ordered, the cups and ice; I've hired the DJ and everything is ready. Brothers will probably start arriving on Friday and start drinking the minute they arrive. This is my first party as president, and since the social chair won't be here until school starts, I'm running things, and I want to impress the brothers as much as I can by making this the best damned party in the history of the chapter. Last year there were only six kegs; this year I ordered ten. The DJ will play until two in the morning, and I've invited all the other fraternities and sororities. The party is an excuse for the brothers to come back to town and hang out for a weekend in the middle of the summer. It started years ago, and it's called the Baby Bash because it's unfair that brothers whose birthdays are in the summer don't get to celebrate them in the house, so we celebrate them all at once in a big blowout of a party. The house is already spotless; I've been getting the other brothers living in the house this summer to help me get it all shipshape.

Usually the house is a disaster area before the party; last year's president thought buying the kegs and hiring the DJ was all he needed to do and then let it go. Not me.

And hangovers or no, everyone is going to get this place cleaned up the day after.

I wonder…no, forget it.

That wouldn't be smart.

"All right, Kenny, are you okay now?" I ask, standing up and smiling down at him. "I have some things to do, but I don't want to chase you out if you still need me."

As I expected, he leaps to his feet awkwardly, all bumbling and clumsy and full of apologies, and can't even get the words out. He's kind of like a puppy, endearing in all of his goofiness, almost adorable in a way.

"No, no, no need to apologize, I'm sorry I have to chase you out," I say, steering him gently through the office and out the door into the hallway. "Are you sure everything's going to be all right with you now?"

He nods, and I smile as I close the door.

I pull my phone out of my pocket. Three hours' time difference between here and Fire Island, so it's late there—I speed-dial Brandon and hit the FaceTime app.

His hair is wet and drops of water are scattered over his face. "What do you want? I just got out of the shower."

"Big plans tonight?"

"We're just going dancing. Dylan is coming with us. Jeff and Blair are here now, too."

"Dylan's going to a club? Isn't he afraid he might be tempted?"

Brandon gives me a sour look. "It's just dancing."

Hmmm, that's an interesting response. Things must not be going well. "I wanted to let you know that I think I've figured out who's been telling Dylan negative intel on you."

That got his attention. "Who?"

"Turns out that Dylan's best friend is Joni Gaylord."

"Gaylord? As in Kenny Gaylord?"

"None other. So Kenny probably talked to her—or she asked him about you."

He gets a lazy smile on his face. "And didn't you say that Kenny is dating Ricky now?"

"Mmm-hmmm."

"I suppose fucking Ricky would be a nice way to punish Kenny for talking out of turn, wouldn't it?"

"You'd really be doing them both a favor," I purr back at him. "You know, they haven't done anything yet. I don't think they know how."

"You always get your way, don't you, Phil?"

"It does seem to work out that way a lot, doesn't it?" I laugh, delighted. "Any luck with your Dylan?"

"Not yet, but we're both coming to the Baby Bash."

"You're going to have a busy weekend, aren't you? Bye, darling." I disconnect the call.

This is working out even better than I could have hoped.

I walk out of my office and up the stairs and knock on Ryan Bradford's door. I can hear rock music blaring from inside. I knock louder.

The door opens and I wince from the loudness of the music. "Is my music too loud?" he yells at me. I shake my head and hold a finger up to my nose, pressing the left nostril closed. Ryan smiles and waves to me to come in. I shut the door behind me and he turns down the music on the stereo system with his iPhone plugged into it. "How much you need?"

Ryan is the house dealer. We all pretend that no one in the house does drugs and that no one in the house is a dealer, but it's how Ryan is paying his way through college. You can never go wrong selling coke and acid and weed to a fraternity, and he does a pretty good business. He's a straight A student, too. He doesn't indulge in his own wares very often—he told me once that's the worst thing any dealer can do, because once you start dipping into your product you're cutting into the profits, and once you start cutting into the profits it's a slow, steady road to bankruptcy, addiction, and rehab.

He should know, his dad is a bankruptcy lawyer who worked his way through school, so all he does is pay Ryan's tuition, and Ryan has to come up with the rest of his money on his own.

"Beats flipping burgers" was all he said when he told me the story.

Ryan also doesn't use the coke to bag chicks, either. "I leave that to my customers. It's a business, man."

I buy a gram from him and he gives me a taster bump.

The coke explodes in my head and I feel light-headed, like I'm floating. It almost tastes like bubblegum, the way the best stuff always does. I check the little origami fold he gives me and it's all rock, too, which means it's as close to pure as I'm going to get. You never can be sure when it's all ground powder.

This should be enough to get me through the weekend and the party, and a little celebratory line tonight won't hurt once I get back to my room, would it?

That's the trick with coke, you can't just give in to it because it will always beat you if you let it. About half an hour or so after I do one line my body will want to do another one, and my mind will start thinking oh just one more won't hurt anything and there's still plenty left and then I'll not want to do it alone and so I'll have to find someone to offer some to and then the next thing you know there's nothing left and I'm licking the paper desperately trying to get a bit more high when the truth is you'll never get more high and the first high is really the only good one and all the rest will do is make your head hurt and your nostrils burn and your eyes tired.

I roll a joint before I grind up a tiny piece of the rock on the framed picture of my parents on my desk. It always makes me laugh a little bit to snort coke off my parents' faces.

I light the joint and take a hit and snort the coke almost immediately.

Perfect. I feel perfect.

I lie back on my bed and think about the party this coming weekend.

Dylan.

What's up with Brandon and that anyway?

I think about the face he made when I made fun of Dylan. That isn't normal. Usually Brandon will go along with just about anything I say, play along with the joke. But he didn't. He made a face and he played it all off.

If I didn't know better, I'd say Brandon was starting to feel something for Dylan Parrish.

Like that's going to happen.

I get out my phone and open the Grindr app.

I need to blow a load.

This party is going to be epic.

BRANDON The music is thumping and I've had more to drink than I should. I'm trying to keep it together, but Dylan, the way he dances! Oh my God, the way he can move that hot little ass and TWERK and who the hell taught this boy how to dance? The dance floor is crowded and Jeff and Blair have already made it more than apparent to me that I'm welcome to join them in their bed tonight, and I might if I can figure out a way to do it without Dylan getting mad or finding out about it, but I am so pissed at Joni fucking Gaylord that I can't wait to get back to San Felice this weekend and fuck her brother's boyfriend.

Damn, it is a small world.

So I am going to fuck her brother's boyfriend and I am going to fuck her best friend.

Although having a three-way with Jeff and Blair…

I look over at them. They're dancing, sweat glistening

on their bodies, and they aren't wearing underwear and I can see the cracks of their asses and how their torsos both have the deep V's from the hip bones down into their crotches, and they are both really good looking and ripped and I know Jeff did porn when he was still in college—I think I may have even seen some of it he has a big dick if I did see it I think it was filmed in Palm Springs and Jordy told me about it and he wouldn't lie and the more I see Jeff the more I think I have seen his porn and I can feel my dick getting hard inside my shorts and the way Dylan is shaking his ass in front of me isn't helping I could just rape that hot little ass here on the dance floor and Jordy is dancing with some Latino-looking muscle boy just to the side of us and this is wonderful, the most fun I've had in a long time and the bumps of coke Blair and Jeff have given me haven't hurt in that regard either although I wish we had some Molly I wonder if Dylan would do Molly and now he's brushing my dick with his hard little ass and my balls are aching and he's now actually grinding into me the little fucking tease and I grab his hips and grind my own crotch against his ass and he looks back over his shoulder and he smiles at me and sweat is pouring down his face and sweat is dripping off my chin onto his back and his skin feels slick and moist and soft with water and now Jeff is behind me and I can feel his dick through our shorts and it's a big one all right it was definitely him and that's all there is to it I am definitely joining them in their room tonight and I am so horny oh my God I could fuck anyone right here and right now and now the lights are coming up as the music stops and it's time to go back to the house.

Jeff whispers into my ear, "Want to join me and Blair?"

I grin back at him and nod, and out of the corner of my eye I can see Dylan has a weird look on his face.

He's jealous.

It's working.

We head back to the house and I go upstairs and down

the hall to Jeff and Blair's room and they are undressing me and both of their mouths are working on my dick and it feels amazing and then Blair is tonguing my ass and my God it feels fantastic and then the poppers are being pushed under my nose and I inhale deeply and my dick gets harder and I can feel my heart pounding in my ears and my dick is straining as Jeff deep-throats it and he is licking the head of my dick and then we are in the bed together and Blair is sucking my dick and Jeff is fucking him in the ass and I put my hands back behind my head and I watch as Blair goes to town and every once in a while Jeff pounds him so hard that my cock pops out of his mouth with a strand of spit connecting the head to his tongue still and he smiles at me and goes back down on me and then we switch again, now I'm fucking Blair while he sucks Jeff and Jeff's dick is horse-like it's so big and the poppers are under my nose again and I'm inhaling and Blair's ass is amazing it feels so good on me and Jeff's dick slips out of his mouth my God that thing is huge and Blair is moaning and breathing hard and then he is blowing a load out onto Jeff's chest and right after that I am coming too and it feels so amazing like the head of my dick is going to blow right off and my balls are going to explode and this is so amazing and now we are both working on Jeff's gigantic dick with our mouths and now he is coming and they are wiping me down with a towel and I pull my shorts back on and they ask me to stay but I shake my head and I step back out into the hallway and the door to Dylan's room is open and he is standing there in the doorway glaring at me and I just shrug and smile back at him and go to my room and shut the door behind me and laugh to myself.

I got off and he's jealous.

He wouldn't be jealous if he didn't have feelings for me.

He will be mine before the end of the summer.

DYLAN I hate to fly. I hate airports.

And I hate traveling with Brandon Benson.

It's been two days since I saw him coming out of Jeff and Blair's room, and the smirk he gave me…God, I'm so stupid.

I can't believe I was starting to think he wasn't everything I'd heard about him.

I'll never doubt Joni again.

I don't know what kind of twisted game he was playing with me, but I don't care.

I'm just glad I now see him for what he is.

I just regret I let him change his flight to San Felice so we would be traveling together.

So now I am stuck with him. We rode the ferry to Sayville together, took the LIRR in to JFK together, and now are sitting in the airport at the gate together. We have a three-hour flight to Houston, then an hour change there, then another four hours to San Felice. We're sitting together on the flights, too. I'm not being rude, I can't be, it's just not who I am as a person, but I am trying to keep the conversation to as bare a minimum as I can.

That smirk. I just can't forget that smirk on his face when he knew I'd caught him.

It makes me itch to punch him.

I'm not a violent person. The way I am reacting to this bothers me.

I guess I don't like being taken for a fool.

I'm usually such a good judge of character, too. I guess that goes to show just how right Joni was about him.

"You're awfully quiet," he says.

"Don't have much to say."

I spent most of yesterday avoiding him with varying degrees of success. The house is big but it's not that big, and I had to eat. I didn't go out to the pool. I didn't need to see Jeff and Blair and Brandon smiling at each other knowingly. I liked Jeff and Blair, they both seemed nice when they first arrived, but how can they do that sort of thing? Don't they love each other?

I don't understand open relationships. I don't think I ever will.

I shouldn't judge, I know. Some of the comments on my monogamy essay at *Out* called me at best a self-righteous puritan, and I will not repeat what the nastier ones said, but they were hurtful. My editor told me to ignore them and not to engage with anyone. It was hard, though, some of the comments were so mean and nasty and personal. But it made me realize what it felt like to be judged. If that was their intent, then it worked. So I shouldn't judge Jeff and Blair. It works for them, great. Life and freedom are about choices, the ability to make choices, and if they choose to bring someone else into their relationship for sex, that's their right.

I just wish it wasn't Brandon.

"You're mad about the other night, aren't you?"

He says it softly, so softly I barely hear it over the hubbub of a crowded airport.

Okay. "I don't have a right to be mad," I say, not looking at him but very aware of how close our bare legs in our shorts are to each other in the waiting area. "You're free to do whatever you want. Or whomever." I can't resist adding that but shouldn't have.

"So why are you being so cold?" His bare leg touches mine briefly but he pulls it away quickly like it's burned. The feel of his skin...no, I can't think like that.

"I'm sorry." I know I don't have a right to be angry. I know I don't, I know that what he does is none of my business, I have a fiancé I love and I'm committed to, I don't care who sleeps with whom. So why?

"Do you have feelings for me?" he asks, his voice still quiet, almost shy.

"No!" I say it louder than I should. People are looking over at us with strange looks on their faces, and I can feel myself blushing in embarrassment. "I mean, I like you, Brandon. You're a nice guy and I hope we can go on being friends."

"That's all you feel for me? Friends?"

"Brandon." I put my hand on his leg. His skin feels hot to my touch, the muscles taut and hard. There's a bit of razor stubble but it doesn't bother me. I know I should take my hand off him but I let it lie there. "I'm engaged. I love Marc more than my own life. We could never be anything more than friends."

He nods, and looks away. "I know. I know and I'm sorry, I didn't want to say anything. But—but I've never felt this way before."

I can't believe he is saying this to me in an airport, where other people can hear. "I don't want to talk about this here," I whisper back to him. "We can talk about it later, when we get to San Felice."

"You promise we will talk about it, though?" He's slumping down in his seat, looks despondent. "You have to promise me."

"Okay, I promise," I reply, not sure how I feel, not sure what's going on with me, can't be certain what I'm thinking.

I can't have feelings for him, can I?

This wasn't the way I felt when I met Marc.

Marc and I were introduced by Joni. He is the older brother of one of her friends at her high school. He was already in college, almost twenty, and I was only seventeen when we met. Marc was so good looking. He was in ROTC at Cal State–Fullerton, so he shaved his scalp bald and worked out three or four times a week. He was a wrestler in high school and played football, too, and came out to his family when he went to college. His family wasn't okay with it yet—well, his parents weren't but his sister Yolanda, Joni's friend, thought it was cool. She was the one who wanted to find her brother a boyfriend, and Joni was the one who came up with the idea of setting us up together. The four of us went out together to dinner at P. F. Chang's and then to see a superhero movie, but I don't remember much about the movie other than there were a lot of explosions and fights and violence and lame jokes and stuff. All I could think about was sitting next to this good-looking guy with the really dark skin and the big brown eyes who made me laugh and our legs were touching and then he reached for my hand and I looked over at him and he was smiling at me, and that was the first time, and then the next time we went out it was just the two of us. And he was understanding, he got it that I didn't want to have sex right away, that it meant more to me than just getting off.

It was so romantic.

We did all kinds of romantic things, and there were times when it seemed like I was living in some romantic movie. We had picnics at the beach, he came to my school dances, and everything was great. Oh sure, there were some racist assholes who tried to hassle us and called him names and called me a race traitor, but we never backed down from them and Marc also taught me how to defend myself, even though I believed in non-violence and always had, but like Marc said, it was okay in self-defense, and the thought of being beaten or something wasn't exactly appealing, and Marc told me that being gay, we should never forget there are people out there who hate us and want to hurt us, but that reality—that reality was something I didn't want to think about but had to. And when the time was right we finally did it. Marc got us a really nice room at a nice hotel and had champagne and roses and chocolate there for me, and when we made love, it was exactly that—making love. It wasn't fucking.

And when he told me he'd enlisted because he couldn't afford school anymore and didn't want to take out loans and was going to be shipping out, I thought my heart had been ripped out of my chest.

He asked me to marry him and I said yes.

I miss him. I miss him every day and worry about him, and

every time my phone rings or I get an email I feel this little tick inside, a tug at my heart, and in the back of my head I wonder if this is going to be the one telling me he's injured or dead or missing. His emails to me and our FaceTime together is so not enough, it's just not, and I am sick at heart every day. And I know I love him, I love him with all of my heart and soul and that's why this whole Brandon thing doesn't compute, doesn't make sense in my head.

I can't love two people at the same time. It's not possible. That's not the way we're wired.

That's not the way I'm wired.

But if I am going to be honest, and I am always honest with myself, the other night dancing at the Pavilion...I started feeling something for Brandon, maybe it was just a physical attraction—he does like to show off that body, and I don't blame him—but dancing with him, we just seemed to connect on a physical plane, and I felt so close to him. When we got back to the house after the bar closed I ran up to my room because I didn't trust myself to be around him anymore, I didn't know what I might do if I didn't get away from him, and that wasn't a good way to feel, I didn't like feeling that way.

I can't do that to Marc.

So I ran up to my room and showered and got into my bed and lay there, staring at the ceiling and listening to the waves outside, but I couldn't sleep. My heart was pounding and my...I was aroused, and I opened up my laptop and pulled up some of the sexy pictures of Marc I keep there just for that reason and I put some lube on my hand and stared at the pictures and thought about how hot and sexy Marc is, but I kept getting images of Brandon in my head, in that skimpy little bikini out by the pool, rubbing suntan oil into his chest and on his muscular legs, and the way he smelled and how he felt rubbing against me on the dance floor and I didn't think about Marc at all anymore, all I could think about was Brandon and how it would feel to have his arms around me and to be in bed with him on top of me and in between my legs and entering me and I wanted him, I wanted him so badly I wanted him to just get nasty, I wanted him to pull my hair and pinch my nipples and slap my face and call me names as he fucked me, I can tell how big he is his bikinis leave nothing to the imagination and he was hard when we were dancing I could feel it behind me and I wanted him I wanted him so bad I wanted him to treat me like his little bitch, I wanted him to control me and dominate me and beg me to fuck me and...

When I was finished I was ashamed of myself.

And then I got back into my bed after cleaning up and just stared at the ceiling, wondering how awful a person I was to even think that way about another man while Marc was risking his life for his country, living in a tent in a horrible place on the other side of the planet while I was on Fire Island fantasizing about getting fucked.

And then I wanted some water and opened my door just in time to see Brandon come out of Jeff and Blair's room.

And smirk at me.

Maybe that was why I overreacted so much? Because I'd just...

"Do you want to get some McDonald's?" he asks, interrupting my thoughts.

I nod. "Sure, I'm starving."

"Can't make a habit of it, though." He gives me a weak smile, wags a finger at me. "Junk food is called junk for a reason."

I smile back at him. "Just this once we'll be bad."

My heart is thumping as we stand up and gather our things.

He must never know how bad I want to be.

PHIL They're waiting for me as I pull up to the curb outside United's baggage claim at the airport.

I put on the flashers and pop the trunk of my car, hopping

out and running around to hug Brandon. He looks amazing, he always does, but the deep tan sets off his blue eyes beautifully, makes them almost seem luminous. He hugs me back tightly and says, "Phil, this is Dylan Parrish. Dylan, this is Phil Connors, our chapter president."

He's short, which I wasn't expecting, and cute if you like that pasty white-haired borderline albino type. I give him a hearty Beta Kappa secret handshake and beam at him. "Welcome to San Felice! We're all very excited to have someone so famous joining us this year. I hope you're going to feel at home with us."

So sweet I almost gag on the sugar, but as president I have a role to play, and this weird-looking little troll's support or vote might be important sometime in the upcoming year.

What on earth does Brandon see in him?

I help them put their bags in the trunk and then close it and jump back into the car before one of the fascist airport police gives me a ticket. Brandon gets into the back, so Dylan gets into the passenger seat. I look at Brandon in the rearview mirror and he has the nerve to wink back at me.

Well, once he sees Ricky he'll forget all about this thing.

I put the car back into gear and pull away from the curb. The airport is actually close to the campus. The fastest way to get to the fraternity house is to turn left when you leave the airport, swing around to the north, and head back west to the campus. But I decide to take the long way, where the traffic is almost always worse—to the west, to give Dylan the ocean view. I'm sure he's been to San Felice before, but it seems like the presidential thing to do.

I ask them about Fire Island and Dylan starts talking in a rush. The sun is hanging in the western sky and he just can't stop talking about how lovely Fire Island was and have I ever been there, do I know Jordy, he's such a nice guy and so on, and not once has he ever mentioned the fiancé. I notice the diamond ring on his left hand and glance back in the mirror at Brandon, who hasn't said hardly anything at all except the occasional agreement or a noncommittal couple of syllables in response to something Dylan has blurted out in his nonstop vocal diarrhea outburst.

Is it possible Brandon has fucked this creature?

He certainly has a shit-eating grin on his face back there as Dylan keeps blathering on.

"I read your piece on *Out* about monogamy," I interrupt him when he stops to breathe again. Thank God for the training I've gotten from listening to the alumni. "And I see your ring. It's quite nice. You must miss Mike."

"Marc," he replies, his face turning red. "His name is Marc."

"I'm sorry!" I say quickly. I notice he gives Brandon a look over the headrest before turning his attention back to me.

Yes, there's something going on there.

"It's okay, it's an easy mistake to make," and now he's off to the races, telling me all about Marc and how much he loves him and how he's off in Afghanistan but they're planning on getting married once he finishes his tour, and then he's going to stay on in San Felice until he graduates and then they'll figure out if he's going to live on base and follow Marc around the globe wherever he's assigned—Marc is apparently planning on a career in the military, how dreary—or get a job and make a home for him in the States.

Finally we're swinging past the campus on Junipero Serra Street, which has the campus on one side and the other side is wall to wall hotels and fast food joints and bars and restaurants and the occasional grocery store and drugstore and everything you can think of. "Are you boys hungry?" I ask as I stop at the red light at the intersection where you turn to go into the campus, with the huge Spanish mission–style campus administration building glaring at us.

"No," Dylan says.

Brandon doesn't say anything so I drive on, making

the turn onto King Fernando Street, or as everyone calls it, Fraternity Row. Most of the houses are on this street, sororities on one side and fraternities on the other. I pull into our parking lot and park in the president's spot. I show Dylan to his room and give him his key, and then Brandon follows me down to my suite.

Once the doors are closed behind us, I pull out my baggie of weed and start rolling a joint. "What on earth do you see in that little boy?" I ask as Brandon stretches out on my bed. "You haven't fucked him already, have you?"

He takes the joint from me and lights it. He exhales and coughs, sips from the can of LaCroix he took from my refrigerator, and smiles at me. "The challenge, of course. You don't think he's attractive?"

This is some good pot, from Humboldt County, sticky with purple hairs. I take a hit and pinch it off. It's too early for me to be incoherent. My entire body relaxes as it takes control, and I feel like I am melting into my chair. "God, this is good shit. And he's a three a.m. fuck at best, Brandon. Admit it, if he wasn't the poster boy for monogamy you wouldn't give him a second look."

"You're such a bitch."

"It's not mean if it's true." I close my eyes and lean back in my chair. I love getting high. It evens me out, calms me down, keeps me from being wound too tightly. Maybe I smoke too much, but it keeps me from ripping people's heads off and shitting down their necks, so there's that. Plus I prefer it to the Xanax, which just always makes me feel like going to sleep. Of course I wake up feeling even so there's that, but smoking pot is just better. It makes me mellow, it allows me to recogize the things that wind me up and make me crazy. "Wait till you meet Ricky. They're not even in the same league."

"Oh, yes, Ricky, that reminds me." He says slowly. I open my eyes and look at him, sprawled over my bed, his shirt riding up so I can see the trail of hair on his stomach leading down to the waistband of his shorts. "I may help you out there after all. Since I'm here and all."

"What changed your mind?" I can't stop myself from smiling.

"You said yourself it was taking Kenny too long. Can't I help out a friend?"

I laugh. "You forget who you're talking to, Brandon."

He opens his eyes and turns his head to look at me. He makes a kissy-face toward me and shrugs. "Kenny's sister Joni is the one who talks shit about me to Dylan. I'd probably already have had him if she wasn't cock-blocking me." He makes a face. "So, I'll pay her back by fucking her brother's boyfriend. It's not my fault her brother is a stammering virgin." He smiles lazily at me. "I'll teach Ricky all my little secrets about how to drive a guy crazy in bed. So, really, I'm doing Kenny a favor."

"I doubt he'll thank you for it." I get a can of LaCroix from the refrigerator for myself. The flavor explodes in my mouth. Another thing I like about getting stoned, everything tastes better. I decide there's no point in telling Brandon that Kenny and his sister hate each other.

Everything is working out so well I can almost relax.

The party's tomorrow.

It might just be the best party ever.

I'm fastening my seat belt.

Bumpy doesn't even being to scratch the surface of what this party will be.

DYLAN I love champagne.

I don't like alcohol. I mean, I'll drink it, but what's the point of it other than to get drunk? And the few times I've been drunk…well, I'm not a fan.

But I love champagne.

I was maybe twelve when I first tasted it, at a cousin's

wedding. After that first time I've never turned it down, and I can't believe Brandon remembered me saying that casually, when we were at the Pavilion that night in Fire Island and he asked me what I wanted to drink. I told him to get me a vodka and cranberry and mentioned I really only liked champagne. And now, the afternoon of the party he's gotten a bottle of champagne for me.

I can't get over how wrong Joni was about him.

I'm a little ashamed of myself, too. I was jealous, even if I won't admit it to him. I was jealous that he was with Jeff and Blair. All I can think of is kissing him, of being in his arms, of being with him the way I shouldn't want to be. He is kind and caring, nothing like the narcissist Joni said he was. He knocked on my door and was gone by the time I opened it to find the bottle of champagne—Veuve Cliquot—with a bow and a card.

The card simply said, *I hope this is okay; maybe we can toast you moving in here tonight? xo Brandon*

It brought tears to my eyes. What a sweet, incredibly thoughtful thing to do.

I put it in my little refrigerator and closed the door.

Joni texted me that she's on her way up from LA with her friend Madison. She didn't say it, but I got the distinct impression she's expecting the two of them to stay in my room while they're here in San Felice. I don't know how I'm going to share the champagne with Brandon with her here. I don't know if I trust myself to go up to his room with the bottle. But if I know Joni she's going to be all over me all night long like white on rice, and I'm not going to get a moment's peace from her and Madison, who I don't even know, and—

Whoa. Joni's my best friend and I haven't seen her all summer.

What is wrong with me?

I lie back down on my bed and stare at the ceiling.

Marc is who I love. Marc is the man I'm going to marry.

Brandon is just a nice guy—

—but I can't stop thinking about him on the dance floor, when I was grinding back on him and I could feel how hard he was and I could smell his sweaty skin and—

Stop it!

—but I can't stop thinking about him, his broad shoulders and his thick arms and those legs, and how he felt through his shorts, and I can see him climbing out of the pool in his tight little yellow bikini wedged between his butt cheeks and the water streaming off his balls, and my hand is creeping down into my shorts and I am closing my eyes and as I stroke myself I can't help it, I can't summon up any image of Marc in my mind, all I can think of is Brandon, Brandon with his crooked grin and the way his leg felt brushing against mine yesterday on the plane and I can feel it, I'm going to come and it's spurting out of me and all over my bare torso and the pain, oh it's so exquisite what is wrong with me...

Marc. I love Marc.

I have to remember that.

It's a good thing Joni's going to be here.

I don't know that I would be able to resist him.

I don't know that I want to.

Oh God, what am I going to do?

BRANDON The champagne was the perfect thing to do.

The party's in full swing, the dance floor is wall to wall sweaty bodies, everyone's getting drunk or getting high or doing lines somewhere, and Joni, that bitch, and her fugly friend Madison have been monopolizing Dylan ever since they got here, they're the kind of girls that make me glad I'm gay, the kind who laugh and squeal in a high-pitched tone that makes dogs howl for miles around and jump up and down when they're excited, and I think I'm going to see if I can point Joey Henderson and his horse dick Madison's way—

she's perfect, the kind of girl he likes to stick it to—and that will get her out of the way.

But Joni's not going anywhere.

She makes me feel sorry for Kenny. I can't imagine having that bitch for a sister. I'd have pushed her in front of a bus or something.

What a bitch.

She thinks she's hot shit, with her little-bitty waist and her perky little boobs with the erect nipples showing through her tank top and her tight shorts and her apple-shaped hard little ass, she's pretty if you're into that preppy sorority slut look with too much makeup and a spray tan, and she's over there dancing, bopping and thinking she's hot shit. She was rude to me, too, when Dylan introduced her to me, and I noticed he was drinking beer in a red cup even though he told me he doesn't like beer and she gave me the stink-eye and I just smiled back at her and she was rude and Dylan noticed and frowned but Madison, her little friend, was friendly enough and it's okay, Joni, you're possessive and protective, but you don't own Dylan's dick.

There's nothing sadder than a straight girl in love with a gay guy.

Dylan's so oblivious he doesn't even realize his "best friend" is in love with him, the pitiful thing, and if she wasn't so determined to cock-block me I'd almost feel sorry for her. But what Dylan does with his dick is none of her fucking business. You're out of your league here, girl.

I see Phil over at the keg, dancing as he gets another beer. I know he's stoned out of his gourd and probably coked up too, and I wonder who he's got his eye on. His shirt is off and he's got a rag or something tied around his head and I watch him as he takes a big drink from his red cup and smiles at someone, and then I see my prey for the night.

Ricky Monterro.

Phil's right, he is even hotter in person than he is in pictures, and that's saying a lot. Ricky just may be the hottest guy at this party. He's got a T-shirt on and shorts and is sweating from being on the dance floor, but the shirt is so wet with sweat it's clinging to him, and damn he's fine, I can't believe he's a virgin, but Catholics will do that to you, and he's smiling and dancing in place and I wonder where Kenny is.

I told Phil to get Kenny wasted so he'd pass out.

It's too early in the evening for that.

I think I'll slip off to my room and do a line, smoke a bowl, refill my cup.

RICKY I think I'm drunk.

I…I kind of like it.

The party is everything I imagined parties to be like, but it doesn't bother me. It doesn't. I know it's supposed to be a sin to drink and dance and everything, but…this is fun. I've only had one beer but my head feels a bit woozy and light and my legs are a bit wobbly, but everything is kind of funny, and I can't stop smiling. The music is pretty loud but I am enjoying this party and am really glad I came here.

This has to have been God's plan for me.

It's so hot I want to take off my shirt like all the other guys have, but I don't know if I should.

Phil is so cute and nice and kind and he is getting me another beer and I don't know where Kenny is but nothing really matters, I know I'll run into him again at some point, right, and I take the beer from Phil and he yells at me over the music, "Take off your shirt!"

"You're wearing yours!"

He smiles and puts his cup down on the beer keg and pulls his T-shirt up over his head, tucks it into the back of his shorts. I just gawk at him for a minute or two. "Wow," I say, shaking my head. "You're in really good shape."

"Thanks!" He laughs back at me, grabs the front of my T-shirt. "Your turn! I did it, now you have to!"

I hesitate.

"It's not a sin, altar boy!" he shouts back at me. "It's not any different than going to the beach."

He's right.

I give him my cup and pull my shirt up over my head and do like he did, tuck it into the back of my shorts. It feels so much better, even though it's hot and sweaty and everyone is dancing and the body heat from the crowd of people out on the dance floor is intense. I've met so many people I'll never be able to remember all their names and I am so glad I'm here, I'm so glad Uncle Rubin talked me into being a Beta Kappa.

I belong here in a way I never did at Notre Dame or high school or even at home.

My eyes fill with unexpected tears because I'm so happy, and Phil hands my beer back to me and asks me if I'm all right and I start to cry and then he grabs me by the arm and rushes me down the hallway and is unlocking his office where it's so cold from the window unit and then we're in his bedroom and he smiles at me and hands me a tissue to dry my eyes.

He kneels in front of me and asks me why I'm crying and he's so concerned and so obviously cares that I start crying even more and he puts his arms around me and holds me and his skin is wet but it's warm and his body his muscles they're solid as rocks and I feel like an idiot but he keeps holding me until I stop and I say I'm okay and he sits back and smiles at me.

"It's the beer," he says gently, still smiling. "You're not used to being tipsy, are you?"

I shake my head. "I've never drank before."

"It can make you emotional." He sits on the edge of his bed, opens his nightstand drawer. "You've never smoked, then?"

He pulls out what I assume must be marijuana. "No."

"Do you want to try?" He holds it in his hand, gets a lighter in his other hand, puts it in his mouth. "I'm going to have some. You don't have to, but don't tell Uncle Rubin." He winks at me and lights it, sucking in. The end flares and a sickly sweet smell fills the room. He blows out an impossibly large cloud of smoke and grins at me.

I put out my hand. "What do I do?"

"You're going to cough, so put your cup down." I did. "Now, you're going to put it in your mouth," he places it in my mouth, putting my fingers on it to keep it in place, "and now breathe in—don't suck, breathe in deeply." I do as he says, and my lungs feel like they are on fire. He takes the cigarette away from me just as smoke starts exploding out of my lungs as I cough and cough, my eyes water and tears streaming down my face and it feels like I'm never going to stop coughing and he smacks me gently on the back, telling me to just keep coughing, go with it and finally I stop and wipe away the tears and my whole body is tingling and my head feels light, like it was barely attached to my body and could float away at any minute, and he hands me my beer and I drink from it and the cold liquid feels good on my throat and I smile at him and finally can say "Wow."

"That was a good hit," he says as he takes another one himself, then pinches it out. He blows out smoke. "How do you feel?"

"Good." I start to giggle because it's funny, everything seems funny to me and I can feel the wind from his window unit on my skin and I can actually feel the goose bumps coming out on my skin and I look at them in wonder, they're amazing how have I never noticed that before and he's saying something and I shake my head which doesn't feel so light anymore now it feels really heavy and my throat feels dry and I take another drink and Phil smiles at me and says let's go back and dance some more and in that moment I love him I love him more than I've ever loved anyone before I want to hug him so I get up and put my arms around him and I tell him I love him and he laughs and says you need to be careful with that you're just high and he's leading me back out of his room and I can hear the music thumping and I thank him and he just smiles at me and we walk back down the hallway and—

KENNY I hate my sister so much.

I think she came to this party specifically to ruin it for me. Her friend Madison isn't much better.

I lost Ricky at some point because she dragged me out of the party and out onto the lawn to lecture me about making sure Dylan stays away from Brandon and I told her to go to hell he's not my problem and she called me an asshole and I told her she was a cunt and she needs to go back to LA and never come back up here again I hate her and her stupid friend and to go fuck herself and now I can't find Ricky anywhere.

I see Phil when I come back inside and I ask him if he's seen Ricky and he says no but he can see I'm upset, so he asks me what's wrong and I say nothing and he doesn't act like he believes me and he says I think Ricky's out on the dance floor why don't you come to my room and we can talk and I say okay and I start crying once we're in there and it all comes pouring out of me and he doesn't laugh at me he just listens and I know I'm making a big fool out of myself but Phil is so kind, he's so very kind I can see why everyone likes him so much and I think maybe I'm too drunk and maybe I need to find Ricky and Phil offers me a joint and I think what the hell and I get high and now I am so wasted everything is spinning and I don't know what to do and Phil puts me into his bed and says to just lie there until everything stops and puts a bucket next to the bed and I don't know why he's being so nice to me and it makes me want to cry and I can't believe I've ruined the whole night for myself and I don't know where Ricky is and all I want to do is cry.

"Shhhh," he says, kissing the top of my head softly. "You're just a little wasted, is all, just lie here and rest for a little while, okay? I'm going to go back out to the party. I'll come check on you in a moment, okay?"

I am so embarrassed I wish the ground would just open and swallow me whole because he is being so nice to me and I don't know what I ever did to deserve it I don't know why I am such a loser and why I let my sister ruin everything for me why did she have to come and where is Ricky and then Phil is closing the door behind him and I put my head in his pillow and just have a good cry and I wish Ricky was with me everything would be so much better if Ricky was here with me but I can't ask him to give up his night because I'm being a baby and having a breakdown and I wish I were dead I do I wish I were dead.

BRANDON There's no way to separate Dylan from his pathetic fag hag and her friend, so I keep my distance. I pointed Joey Henderson in Madison's direction and he's dancing with her. If I didn't know he was a straight boy, just watching him dance... You'd think a swimmer would have some sense of rhythm, but Jesus fucking Christ, the way he dances is a hate crime. Little Miss Madison is going to get boned by Joey by the end of the night if I'm not mistaken, and I'd find someone to fuck the fag hag but it's pretty clear the only dick she's interested in is one she's not going to get.

But she's sure as hell not going to let anyone else have it, either.

I bet she hates Marc. I bet she's polite to him and makes nice while she seethes and waits for the chance to break them up. God she's pathetic, and she would never in a million years admit she's in love with him but somehow thinks no one else can notice.

Oh, I'm on to you, Miss Fag Hag. I've seen your type before. And before I'm done with you, you won't even know what happened. You're done. You're not going to keep cock-blocking Dylan for the rest of your life.

I wonder if she does coke.

Ryan Bradford is doing some good business tonight, I bet. Plenty of people dancing with that clenched jaw or rubbing their noses, and maybe it's time for me to do another line since I'm not going to fuck Dylan tonight, which is fine—I know how to play this; it's so damned predictable it would be sad if it weren't so easy and funny—he'll want to know why I stayed away from him all night and I'll say his Fag Hag, who I will have to call Joni, I can't call her Fag Hag to him or maybe I can, I'll have to see how it works out but I'll let him know she made it clear I wasn't welcome to hang out around them, and in fact, before I go find little Ricky and make him a man tonight I'll dance over there so she can be a bitch to me so he can see it for himself.

Stupid little fag hag, you can never outplay a fag.

I head over to the kegs to get another beer. I see Phil coming back across the foyer with a shit-eating grin on his face and he meets me at the keg. I haven't seen him in a while so I ask him where he's been and he winks at me and says, "I got Kenny wasted and put him to bed in my room, so the coast is clear for you," and this is exactly what I mean, little fag hag. You will always get outplayed by a gay man.

Always.

"Thanks," I say as I get another beer and hand him the tap. I take a drink and wink at him. Time to show Dylan what a bitch his little hag really is. "Watch this."

The dance floor is crowded and the deejay has moved into his 1980s greatest hits set, which always starts with Billy Idol's "Mony Mony," which I am sick to death of listening to,

and then it will be the Go-Go's and the Romantics and Dead
or Alive and everyone will dance and sing along like they're
the first people to know these songs or shout *hey hey what get
laid get fucked* between every line of Billy Idol, and I roll my
eyes as I work my way around drunk and stoned and coked
dancers and try not to slip on the beer-slick floor and it's so
hot out there from all the body heat that I start sweating all
over again and can feel sweat running down in the crack of
my ass because I'm not wearing underwear, and I know my
shorts are riding low and people can see the top part of my ass
but that's okay because I want them to and some dopey blond
bitch runs her hand down my chest as I walk past her and I
smile at her and keep going where Dylan is dirty dancing with
the hag and Joey is grinding on Madison and she's got that
glazed look in her eyes because she can't believe someone as
hot as Joey wants to fuck her so she's going to put out the way
ugly girls will always put out to a hot guy because they have
no self-esteem and they think fucking a hot guy will somehow
magically turn them into a hot chick.

And then I move around Joey and Madison, and Dylan
sees me and he smiles and turns his back to me and wiggles
his ass and I know he wants me to grind on him wants me to
dry-hump right there on the dance floor and I see the anger flit
across the hag's face for a moment and she gets in between us
pretending like she's dancing and not doing what she is really
doing and I just give her a weird look instead of laughing in
her face and turn to Joey and Madison and start dancing with
them and Joey yells "DUDE" right in my face and he reeks of
sweat and pot and sour beer and we high-five each other and
start dancing around Madison with me in front of her and him
behind her and he's grinding on her fat ass and I'm bumping
and grinding and smiling at her and she puts both her wet
hands on my chest and she looks dazed and I know she's died
and gone to heaven and if I was into that, me and Joey could
take her back to his room and we could both have her and

she'd be into it the way the not-so-pretty girls always are, and for a minute I think about it because I know Joey likes having his dick sucked so I could suck his dick while I fuck her and I could pretend she was a dude but I know I'm just high and drunk and horny and the last thing I'm ever sticking my dick into is a pussy.

Been there done that, no thank you.

Dylan turns around and looks confused because he was expecting me to be grinding on him and I'm not and he doesn't understand why the hag is there instead of me and he meets my eyes and I just shrug and make an I-don't-know face and he doesn't look happy and I shrug again and kiss Madison on the top of her sweaty head and high-five Joey again and make my way off the dance floor, and when I get to the big doorway to the foyer I look back over and Dylan is not happy and he is talking to the hag excitedly and she's acting all defensive and this is a good time for me to duck out to my room for a line. I head down the hallway and put the key in my door and open the door and go inside and wipe myself down with a towel because I am soaked and I drop my shorts off and dry my ass and my balls and sit down at my desk naked and open the top drawer where I keep my mirror and there's a little pile of coke on the side and I spread it out with my ATM card and make a line and pick up the hollowed-out pen and suck it all up in my right nostril and it explodes in my head and it tastes kind of like bubblegum and I feel my entire body tingling again and I pull out my little pipe as I can taste the drip on the back of my throat and I take a big hit off the pipe and exhale and when I'm finished coughing I take a drink of my beer and put the mirror back away after rubbing the residue on my gums to numb them and I close the drawer and I get up and look at myself in the mirror.

I look fucking hot.

I'd totally fuck me.

My dick is getting hard.

Some guys think coke gives you limp dick, but that's never been a problem for me.

I'm horny and I need to get laid.

I find another pair of shorts and pull them on. I drain my beer and put my key in my front pocket and head back out to the party.

I'm in luck because as soon as I close my door, Ricky stumbles through the swinging doors from the bathroom and he's got a silly look on his face, goofy, and he's lost his shirt at some point and he is hot, Phil was right, and my dick is getting harder and he gives me his goofy grin and stumbles down the hallway to me and puts both of his hands on my chest and says, "hey there, I think I'm wasted," and I say, "yeah you kind of are, come on, let's sit in my room for a minute," and I unlock the door and steer him pretty easily to the bed and he falls down onto it and starts giggling and I tell him to not move I'm going to go get us both a beer and I can't believe how easy all of this is, he just literally dropped into my lap but I'm not one to question fate or whatever the hell you want to call it, and I head back into the foyer and have to wait a minute for my beers behind some of my brothers who are wasted and probably should be cut off but it's their hangover not mine and they're shouting PARTY and WOO HOO at me and I smile back at them as they head back out onto the dance floor and now it's the Romantics and "What I Like About You" and I wonder if the same deejay has been playing these songs at Beta Kappa parties since they were like actually hits being played on the radio and I don't understand straight people at all they'd probably be pissed if these songs weren't played and I carry the beers back down the hall and don't bother to look for Dylan and the Hag because I don't care the damage is done I planted the seeds and if there's any luck in the world they won't be speaking by the end of the night and she's going to call him a whore at best and it's not my problem, is it?

I kick the door closed behind me and Ricky is still lying

on his back on my bed staring at the ceiling and he picks his head up and smiles at me and I put his beer on the nightstand for him and wonder how direct I can be. I decide to play it cool and get my pipe out of my drawer and sit down on the bed beside him, and he rolls up to sit next to me. He's right on top of me, our legs touching, and he's leaning on me and he asks me if that's pot.

"You want some?" I ask. "You've smoked pot before?"

He nods animatedly and says, "I had some earlier for the first time ever and I really like it and I want to have some more."

And I almost feel sorry for him, he's so wasted and he is pretty. He has such pretty skin and those deep dimples in both cheeks and long curling lashes on his eyes and thick lips and he has no idea where this is going to go.

Or does he?

He's been pushing down his sexuality his whole life and using the Virgin Mary and the Lord Jesus to do it.

He's probably going to blow a huge load and he's going to like it.

And I remember the hag and her brother and yeah, I'm going to go through with it. I take a hit and pass the pipe to him. "You know how to smoke from a pipe?"

"You put it in your mouth and you suck on it," he says and starts laughing, pleased with himself.

Oh, yeah, he's ready for it, all right.

"Inhale, not suck. If you suck it you'll choke. Like this." I demonstrate again. I am pretty wasted myself, the beer and the coke and the pot are all combining to make my head hazy, but I still know what I'm doing but give me another hour and I'll be too wasted to do anything. I hold the pipe to his mouth and flick the lighter. "Inhale," I say and he does, closing his eyes and inhaling, a huge hit that is going to knock him on his ass and sure enough he starts coughing and smoke is coming out of his mouth and his nose and I put the pipe down on the nightstand and hand him his beer and he takes it and drinks about half of it down and burps and then looks sheepish and guilty and says "Sorry" and he starts laughing and he falls back on the bed and I lie down next to him and ask him if he's having a good time and he says yes and I lean over and look into his eyes and he looks back and he actually tilts his head up and kisses me.

Yeah, he's fucking ready.

And I lean down and kiss him back, and he tastes like smoke and sour beer and toothpaste and I push my tongue into his mouth and he grips it with his mouth and sucks on my tongue and it feels good if surprising and I think *where did he learn to do that* and then he is pushing me back down onto my back and rolls his sweaty muscled body on top of mine and is pushing his tongue into my mouth and grinding his crotch against mine so I put my arms around him and let my hands cup his big round hard ass and he moans a little bit as he keeps grinding and I roll him over and now I am on top of him and I can feel his hard-on through his shorts and I move my mouth to his ear and nibble on the lobe and he is moaning and grinding and thrusting his hips and his eyes are closed and I run my tongue down the side of his wet throat and taste his salt and he is liking this a lot and I reach the hollow at the base of his throat and work my way down to his left nipple, swirling my tongue around it as it gets harder.

I hear him say "what are you doing" in his drunken stoned stupor and I stop and look up at him and say "I'll stop if you want me to" and he says "no no no don't ever stop" and his head drops back on the pillow and I keep teasing the nipple, nipping it a bit with my teeth which makes his body convulse so he clearly has sensitive nipples and so I put my hand on his right one and start pinching it gently and he's moaning and he's liking this a lot and my guess is once he gives into it he's going to love it and be pretty damned insatiable like they always are and he probably would never admit it, it being a sin and all, but he probably beats off several times a day and every once in a while he looks down at me and he's having a great time but I can see he's nervous so I stop working his nipple with my teeth and whisper "it's okay to like this, Ricky, you know" and his eyes well up with tears and he nods and the tears start slipping out of his eyes and I kiss him again, softly and gently, and slip my arms around him and hold on to him, not applying any pressure with either my arms or my mouth and I kiss his tears away and he is sniffling and he whispers "I've wanted this for so long" and I kiss his mouth and whisper into his ear "then enjoy it, Ricky, there's nothing wrong with enjoying it" and I can see the dam in his mind holding him back break and his hands run down my back and now he's grabbing my ass and then they are exploring my back, like he's always wanted to know what a male body feels like and then he is holding my biceps and asks me to flex for him and I smile down at him and sit up and flex my arms, tightening my abs and my shoulders, and he runs his wondering hands down my body, feeling the muscles, and his touch on my damp skin, so light and graceful, is making my dick harder and my balls ache, but as much as I want to rush this, tear off his shorts and tilt his hips up and just fuck him as hard as I can, I can't do that to him.

The innocent wonder on his face.

Stupid fucking Catholics have done a number on him.

I wonder how many priests have—

Don't go there, Brandon.

"You like how that feels?" I whisper and he nods. I run my fingertips down his torso from the base of his neck to his navel, brushing the skin lightly and he shivers, goose bumps rising on his arms, and he clamps his lips together and another tear runs out of his left eye and I lean down and kiss the tear away. I slide back down the bed and stick my tongue into his navel, which tastes like sweat and soap, and pinch both of his nipples lightly then harder and he groans and his lower back arches up and now the crotch of his shorts is rubbing against my chest and I slide my fingers down and unfasten his shorts and pull the zipper down and he's whimpering now but he lifts his ass up as I slide the shorts down and off.

His white briefs are soaked through with sweat, clinging to his uncut erection, which is straining against the wet cotton and he looks up at me, pleading with his eyes.

"We can stop now if you want to," I say, knowing he won't want to stop.

He gets up on his knees and walks on them down to the foot of the bed. He fumbles with the snap of my shorts with a knowing smile on his face. I put my arms around him and pull him into my body, our chests crushing together, and I slide my right hand inside the back of his underwear, my index finger slipping down between the hard cheeks, past the hairs inside them, and both cheeks clench together as my finger reaches the promised land.

"Relax," I whisper.

"I—I've never—"

"I know," I say, nuzzling on his neck again, "I'll be gentle."

With my other hand I unzip my shorts and they fall to the floor. I kick them off and press my bare cock against his, and he is shivering again. I pull his underwear down to his knees as he unclenches his cheeks and I tap my finger against his hole. He shivers again and I kiss him again, and this time he moves his lips down from mine to my neck, kissing and licking the tender skin there and now it's my turn to moan, and he shifts on the bed and his underwear is off and on the floor and I push him backward, lowering him down to his back with me on top of him and then I'm startled as he starts licking my cock, running his tongue up and down the shaft, takes the head into his mouth and swirls his tongue around it like a pro and I wonder how he knew to do that but porn is everywhere, he must have watched some on the internet, and I take his cock in my hand and run my thumb over the head and some precum leaks out and I smear it over the head and keep running my thumb over it while he licks mine and I still am tapping his hole with my other index finger and I look over his body and he is magnificent, Phil was right, the body is without flaw and he knows enough to mimic what I am doing with his cock and we smile at each other and we lie back down on the bed together and kiss gently while we masturbate each other slowly, even though I have to be careful since he's never done this before, he might blow his load too soon but he's a willing pupil and there's no doubt in my mind that this is just the first time we're going to do this together and even though I hate teaching people he is going to be a wonderful pupil...

RICKY oh my God this feels so amazing it's even better than I could have ever imagined it to be I've beaten off before but having someone else do it to me is a whole other thing I feel like I'm going to explode and his is so big I want to suck him I want him inside me but I don't know if I can handle him he's so big and I've never done this before oh my God this is so amazing—

BRANDON ...and then I take him in my mouth, and I start sucking him, cupping his heavy balls with my other hand and I start moving up and down and I know he's close, he's going to come really soon but that's fine we have all night and I bet he'll be able to get it back up again without a problem and he's grabbing my head with both hands, I was right, and sure enough I pull my head back and he's shooting gobs into my face and he's moaning so loud if it weren't for the stereo system at the party everyone in the house would hear him and I just smile until he stops shuddering and shaking and the last bits dribble out of him and I reach for a towel and wipe my face down and I touch the head of his dick with my finger and he flinches but the erection is still there, maybe a bit softer and not quite as driven as before and he's telling me he's sorry and I smile at him and lie down next to him, put my arm around him and curl his head down onto my shoulder and kiss his sweaty curls and say "no worries, we have all night and there's plenty of time" and he looks up at me with his pretty eyes and says "I want to make you come" and I smile back at him and say "I want you to" and so I teach him the basics of cocksucking and he's not great but he's not bad for his first time and I know he's not going to make me come but we have all night...

DYLAN I haven't seen Brandon in a long time. The party's winding down now and there aren't as many people dancing as there was earlier and I am drunk, more drunk than I want to be but the dancing made me hot and thirsty, so I kept drinking. Madison's missing, too, she went off with Joey what's-his-name a while ago and I guess she's getting fucked, good for her I guess, but I kind of wish Joni would have found someone, too.

Why have I never noticed before that her attachment to me doesn't seem normal?

She always calls us Will and Grace, but I don't want to have a straight wife, which was always the problem for me with that show, you know, it was great that they were friends but that they were more important to each other than any potential partners and always chose the other over Grace's husband or Will's boyfriends just wasn't normal and now I am wondering if that's what Joni wants from me? I mean, now that I think back over it, Marc was the only person she never had a problem with me dating, and we always knew Marc was going to be going away to serve, so was that why she was okay with it, because she knew he was going to be leaving and I don't know I shouldn't have had so much to drink but why is

she so obsessed with who I sleep with instead of finding her
own boyfriend?

I shouldn't be thinking this way Joni has always been
there for me, hasn't she?

Or has she been hindering me?

Why am I even wondering about this?

I don't want to dance anymore.

"I'm going to my room," I shout to her over some Justin
Bieber remix that should be banned from ever being played.

She nods and obediently walks with me out of the big
room and down the hall and I am annoyed because it's like
she's a fucking puppy who can't let me out of her sight and she
says "I got to pee wait for me" and disappears inside the girls'
bathroom and for a minute I think I should keep walking and
go to my room and lock the door and then pretend like I don't
hear her pounding on the door she can sleep in her brother's
room why does she always have to be around me and she kind
of invited herself and Madison to this party in the first place
it's not like I had any say in this and Madison is supposed
to be one of her best friends but she doesn't even care that
we haven't seen Madison in like forever and she's getting her
brains fucked out by some guy SHE JUST MET and Joni is
somehow fine with that but she has to police every guy I've
ever been interested in and it's none of her fucking business
in the first place and I think maybe I should just walk down
the hall and knock on Brandon's door and spend the night
with him and then I can't believe I am even thinking this way
what the hell is wrong with me I am not going to sleep with
someone just to teach Joni a lesson and this is why I probably
shouldn't drink and maybe living in the house where Brandon
is might be a mistake and maybe I should think about getting
an apartment near campus and just avoid parties here and here
she comes stumbling out of the bathroom and she is giggling
and I know she's pretty wasted too and I am just sick to death

of her and wish she hadn't come if she hadn't come I'd be with Brandon maybe right now and—

I have to stop thinking about that. I am in love with *Marc* and I am going to marry *Marc* and he's off risking his life serving our country and I am a terrible person and—

But is it so wrong to want to be with Brandon? Is it?

I don't know what the hell is wrong with me.

And I walk up the stairs to my room and she's babbling about nonsense and not even making sense and I can smell her and she smells like sour beer and sweat and perfume cheap and cloying and her makeup is smeared all over her face and she's just, I don't know, I don't understand, I don't know what the hell I'm thinking, she's my best friend and I love her and she's always been there for me but I can remember in high school when I was crazy about Danny Winters and he was interested in me and she told me all kinds of bad things about him under the guise of protecting me and I had a right to know what kind of person Danny Winters was and I shouldn't be wasting my time with someone like that and who the hell is she to make those decisions for me she's been doing that my whole life and what kind of friend does that she just wants me to herself and isn't that why you transferred from UCLA in the first place?

Isn't that the deep dark secret truth you'd never admit to anyone before?

It had nothing to do with staying in LA reminding me too much of Marc and being sad, you wanted to get away from Joni so she could get her own life and stop suffocating you.

She is blabbing now as I unlock my room about how much she loves this house and it's such a better chapter than the one at UCLA and San Felice is so much better than Westwood and maybe she should transfer her too and—

"No, you shouldn't," I say, tossing my keys into the mug on my desk where I always keep them so I don't ever lose them. "San Felice is my place and your place is there."

She's staring at me and I can the tears forming in her eyes, this is what she always does, how she always manipulates me into giving in to her demands and her needs, she always starts crying because it bothers me I hate to see anyone cry but the beer has given me resolve and I'm going to stand up to her for once. "Don't you want me here so we can, you know, hang out like we always have?" and her voice is quivering and her lower lip is trembling and the manipulation is coming and I am not going to have it.

"No," I reply, sitting down on my bed and feeling very brave and proud of myself. "I think you need to stay at UCLA and get a life of your own."

"Don't you miss me?"

"You aren't listening to me," I say and it's all bubbling up inside me now, and I know I can't say what I'm feeling it's too mean and cruel but if I don't stand up for myself now I'll be trapped forever. "I don't want to be Will anymore. I have Marc." I gesture around the room. "I have a new house full of new brothers to meet, a whole new life, and you need to do the same."

"Why are you being so mean?"

"Where's Madison?"

That stuns her, catches her off guard. "Madison? What does she have to do with this?"

"You don't even know where she is. You don't even care. She could be getting gang-raped in the chapter room and it's never even occurred to you to wonder where she is."

Her mouth opens and closes.

"You're always lecturing me on what a bad friend I am when I don't do what you want me to"—the words are all tumbling out of me now, and I should maybe stop but I don't, I need to say these things to her, they've been building up inside me for so long that I feel like if I don't clear the air and make it clear to her what exactly she's been doing I never will and then I'll be trapped forever—"but look at the kind of friend *you* are. Where's Madison? Do you even care? No, you don't, you just dragged her up with you uninvited, you never even thought to ask me if it was okay for you to come and bring her, no you just assumed like you always do that you're welcome and it never even crosses your mind that maybe just for once you aren't and maybe I'd like to hang out here and meet the brothers and party with them and get to know some of them since I literally just got here yesterday but no you have to come barging in like it's your goddamned fraternity house and then you cling to me all goddamned night and all you ever do is try to control me and who I can be friends with and like Brandon Benson you couldn't wait to tell me all kinds of bad things about him and maybe I'd like to make up my own mind about someone for once but you just can't let me because what, you think because I'm gay I'm too stupid?" I stop for breath and her face is shocked, like I've slapped her and I guess it's kind of like I have because no one has ever stood up to her before.

Her face twists into a nasty sneer. "Brandon Benson. Is that what this is really about?"

"It's none of your fucking business if it is."

"You're going to cheat on Marc." She's gathering her self-righteousness around her like a cloak now, and starting to get her controlling bitch on. "You want to fuck Brandon, isn't that what this is? Well, go ahead and throw your future with Marc away if you want to!"

"I never said that I wanted to fuck Brandon. And if I want to throw my future with Marc away, news flash: it's my fucking future to throw away, not yours. And if I want to, or if I want to fuck Brandon or I don't, it's none of your fucking business in the first place. Who I sleep with is none of your fucking business!"

"I'm your friend and I care about you—"

"You don't care about anyone except yourself."

"That's a terrible thing to say! Do you really believe that?"

She's breathing hard now and her face is red. This is where I'm supposed to apologize and blame being drunk but I'm not going to because it feels good, it feels good to finally tell her the truth. Just because we get along and have a similar sense of humor and enjoy the same movies and TV shows and think the same actors and singers are hot and like to laugh at the Kardashians and the real housewives doesn't mean I want to spend the rest of my life being controlled and manipulated by a straight girl who's in love with me.

And that's really what this is all about it. She's in love with me and she can never have me so she settles for this weird twisted Will-and-Grace thing when what I'd rather have is a Karen to my Jack.

"No, I don't," and even through my own anger and the haze of the alcohol I'm being gentle with her, "I think you care too much about me. You need to step back and let me live my life, Joni. And you need to live yours."

Tears spill out of her eyes. She wipes them away. "Fine. I will." She grabs the doorknob. "Have a nice life, Dylan Parrish. And someday you're going to need me and I'm not going to be there."

The door slams behind her.

I know I'm supposed to run after her, apologizing and begging her to forgive me, but I don't. That's not how this episode of the soap opera that's Joni's life is going to play out, and I'm finished being her courtier.

I lie back on my bed.

I feel…free.

It *is* my life, after all.

I don't know what I want. I love Marc, I still want to marry him and I don't want to hurt him, but…at the same time, he chose to go into the military. Would it be fair to him to stay with him out of obligation rather than because I love him and want to spend the rest of my life with him?

I wouldn't want him to stay with me that way.

I'm confused and I need to figure this all out.

But Joni wouldn't have helped, and not because she had my best interests in mind.

She hasn't in a long time, if she ever did in the first place.

The kindest thing I could do for her is stop being her friend, stop being around her, stop letting her think in her wildest dreams I would spend the rest of my life with her. She needs to get over her obsession with me and find some nice guy.

And Madison is her responsibility, not mine.

I need to talk to Marc.

I owe him honesty.

Otherwise, whatever we have is over already.

I close my eyes.

RICKY "You need to relax," he whispers in my ear, his lips brushing against it and making my whole body shiver again. "Can you do that?"

I am lying on my stomach and he is kissing the back of my neck and running his tongue down my spine and then his mouth is between my butt cheeks, kissing me, darting his tongue into my asshole, and I have never felt like this before, I never knew it was possible to feel this good and I am so glad I gave up the priesthood I don't want this to ever end and Brandon's taking me to places I never knew I could go, making me feel pleasure I'd never imagined or dreamed was even possible, and his hand slides under me and grabs my aching dick again and I am shuddering and shivering and then a finger is tapping at my asshole again and I want him inside me, I do but at the same time I'm afraid, I've never done something like this before, and I can feel the pressure against it and I close my eyes because it hurts a bit and it feels good at the same time and he's whispering "relax don't worry I'll go slow I don't want to hurt you" and I feel so safe and I know he cares about me I know he knows what he's doing but I'm not sure what he means by relax so I try really hard I let my muscles go limp and then I tense up as the pressure increases and I cry out and everything goes tense again and my eyes open oh my god he can't be serious how does anyone do this and I can hear him whispering "relax baby it's okay take your time and get used to it I won't force you" and his fingertips are brushing against my lower back and I don't know if I can do this and he says "if you tell me to stop I will" but even though I'm afraid I don't want him to stop and I try again and then I feel it, he's inside me and it's an odd feeling I've never felt this way before and it hurts but it also feels kind of good and he's gentle, oh-so-gentle and moving inside me a little bit at a time and I can't believe it's happening I can't believe he is doing it and I—

Oh my god oh my god this is amazing I've never oh my god I want him inside all the way inside I want to take all of him I want him to ride me a little bitch I want him to own me and make me his oh my god oh my god

BRANDON He likes it.

I smile to myself.

I had a feeling he would.

I'm almost all the way inside now.

I want to shove my dick all the way inside, I want to fuck him hard and long and stretch him out like an old whore and just pound that beautiful ass, he looks so beautiful there under me, his beautiful big thick bubble muscle ass spread wide and curved and the muscles in his back and shoulders rippling as he trembles and shivers in pleasure and I want to slap his ass and call him names, make him beg me to fuck him, but this time has to be about trust...

He'll beg to be my little fuck bitch soon enough.

His ass is tight but it feels like velvet inside, the way it's closing around my cock and holding on to it, I actually have to stop because if I don't I'll come and it's too soon, but his ass feels amazing and I am definitely going to fuck this boy again.

And I push the last little bit inside him.

He reaches back with both hands and arches his back up and grabs hold of my ass.

He was born to be fucked.

PHIL The party was a huge success.

I should smoke some pot, get really stoned and fall asleep but I'm in the *I want* stage with the coke so I take the mirror out of my desk and do up another fat line. Usually when I get to this point I don't because that's how the coke takes over, how it takes control, you give in to the impulses and the need and it's not smart, you don't really need more and you're never going to get that original high back but I am celebrating and the key is just not to buy any more and there's really not any point in saving what I have left but is that just rationalizing but the truth is I bought more coke than I needed because I thought Brandon and I would spend the night partying tonight and so I bought some for him but he decided he wanted to fuck someone more than he wanted to hang with me and that's fine.

That's why we aren't a couple.

Brandon is a little like coke, I realize as I roll up a twenty dollar bill and snort the fat line up and tilt my head back, run my index finger over the debris and rub it on my gums.

Kenny is asleep on my bed, his mouth open and some drool running out of the corner. He's kind of cute, not usually the kind of guy I go for, I'd probably swipe left on him on Grindr, but he's sweet and kind of innocent and I feel bad for him. That sister of his is some piece of work, that's for sure.

I finish my beer and decide to head out to the kegs to get one more cup, my head feels light and I see that the DJ is packing up and there's still some people around, wasted out of their minds and the dining room floor is covered in muddy beer and I get another beer and head back to my room and I see Kenny's sister's friend what's her name stumble out of Joey Henderson's room and she looks wasted and her T-shirt is on inside out and she just grimaces at me and her makeup is all smeared and her hair is a mess and she runs up the stairs and I go back to the office and back into my room and he's still snoring and I lock the door behind me and sit down.

Brandon is like coke, his big dick. I remember the first time we were together, oh my God, when he was fucking me I couldn't believe how he made me feel, it was so amazing and we had so much fun and we pretty much spent the entire weekend fucking and sucking and getting high and by Sunday my nipples and ass and dick were so sore I couldn't stand to have them touched and we'd been taking turns fucking each other and his ass I've never fucked anyone the way I fucked Brandon that weekend but I also knew it was never going to work with us because we were so much alike and if we tried to make it work I knew I'd eventually hate him and he'd eventually hate me and I didn't want that and neither did he so we closed those feelings off and became friends and kind of just enjoyed watching each other's tricks and games and living vicariously through each other because I know Brandon will never fall in love and he knows I never will either and someday we'll both graduate but I think we'll be friends, we'll always be friends and we'll always compare notes.

Love is for suckers. Look at his stupid Dylan, for example. Love only works when the two people aren't appealing to anyone else, right? I mean, once someone attractive starts showing you some attention or distracts you away from the person you love, you'll cheat and it's over. I've watched this happen with straight people all the fucking time. My dad cheats on my mother every once in a while and she just pretends it doesn't happen because she doesn't want to know about it, because if she does she would have to do something about it and she doesn't want to get a divorce and be alone for the rest of her life and it's sick and sad, like there's some kind of crime, some kind of shame, in being alone?

I'd rather be alone than be with someone who is going to treat me that way.

I refuse to be a laughingstock like my mother.

And there are brothers here who have fiancées who go to other schools or live somewhere else and they fuck around on them all the time and then blame getting drunk and we're all supposed to pretend it never happened when the fiancées are around, we're all supposed to pretend like they're faithful and all that "bros before hoes" shit, which makes me sick. I'd want to know if I was being made a fool of.

And Brandon agreed with me after that weekend was over, he knows what he is, he knows what I am, and we both knew it would never work and so we remained friends.

Maybe in a different time, maybe in a different world, we could have made it work.

But this world isn't that world.

I couldn't be faithful to him any more than he could have been faithful to me.

I mean his whole thing with Dylan? This is about proving there's no such thing as true love and fidelity, isn't it, proving the way we see the world is right?

I want to believe it, or is it the coke? I sip my beer and take another hit from the pipe.

This is why I don't like to get this wasted.

My mind goes to weird places, places I don't want to go, thinks things I don't want to think, never want to admit to, brings up feelings I don't want to have.

I pity any fool who falls in love with Brandon.

I pity any fool who falls in love with me.

RICKY I didn't think it was possible to feel this way.

I came twice while he was inside me and now I'm lying

in bed curled up with Brandon. I can't help myself, I say that I love him.

He laughs and kisses the top of my head. "You don't love me, Ricky, you're just feeling close to me because you I made you come a couple of times. There's a difference between sex and love, Ricky, and don't ever mistake the two."

"But—"

He puts his index finger on my lips. "Shhh. You don't love me, Ricky, you barely know me. Do you think you can fall in love with someone you barely know? What about Kenny?"

Kenny.

I sit up in the bed, cover my face in my hands, shamed. "I'm a terrible person."

He traces a finger down my spine, and my body reacts, shivers, goose bumps come up, and my—my dick starts to stir again. "You're not a terrible person, Ricky, you've just always been taught that sex is the same thing as love, and that's wrong."

"But I love Kenny, or at least I thought I did." I'm confused. How can I love Kenny when I didn't even think about him when all this was happening?

How can I love Kenny when I want Brandon to do it all to me all over again?

He takes a hit from his pipe and offers it to me. I know I shouldn't, getting drunk and high was part of what caused this to happen—

No, I did this. I can't blame alcohol and drugs.

I'm responsible for what I do.

Well, I'm already going to hell, so I take the pipe from him and inhale. My whole body starts to relax as I blow the smoke out and I lie back into him, his arm around my shoulders, and rest my head on his chest. His dick is hard again, and I hope that means—

"You can love Kenny and have sex with me," Brandon says. "The two things aren't mutually exclusive. We just won't tell Kenny about it, is all. Besides, you don't want your first time to be with someone who doesn't know how to do it, do you?"

I think about it. I'm high, the buzz from the beer is starting to go away but my mind is cloudy, what he's saying shouldn't make sense, it goes against everything I believe, but somehow it does make sense.

And I want him again.

Is that why it makes sense?

Am I justifying what I've done? What I want to do again?

I don't have anyone to talk to about this. I know what a priest would say. Kenny…he's right, I can't tell Kenny, so I can't talk to him about this. Uncle Rubin wouldn't understand. Sergio and Lupe wouldn't, but they're straight and they're all about one person.

Being gay is different. I really am understanding that now.

The same rules don't apply here.

And I know he's right. Kenny wouldn't have known to be so gentle, wouldn't have known to tell me to relax. It wouldn't have been nearly this nice, wouldn't have felt this good, wouldn't have left me wanting to do it again the way this did.

"Kenny might not understand," he is saying, and he kisses the top of my head again. "And you love him, and he loves you. You don't have to tell him until you think he can handle it. And you two haven't exactly decided that you are committed to each other only, have you?"

"No."

"So, unless you've decided not to see other people, you haven't done anything wrong."

It—it makes sense, or does it just make me feel better?

I'm so confused.

"Tell you what," he purrs in my ear, "this time I'll let you fuck me, so you can see how that feels." He leans down and sucks on my left nipple and my eyes close and I'll do anything he wants me to.

I nod. "Yes, yes, please." I barely breathe the words out, and he is slipping a condom on me and straddles me, grabbing me with his hand to guide it inside him, and his body above mine is so amazing, like something Michelangelo would have carved, like all the paintings I've studied and the muscles and the veins bulging and his eyes close as he lowers himself down onto me, and it feels so great, and I can't stop looking at him as he starts riding me, squirting some lube on himself and sliding his right hand back and forth as he rides me...

I don't want this to ever end.

Oh my God...

PHIL I open the door and Brandon is standing there with a shit-eating grin on his face and a greasy bag from Carl's Jr. in his hand.

"We're not supposed to eat there because they're homophobic," I say as I let him in and close the door behind him.

It's after noon and I finally fell asleep around six, after waking Kenny up and sending him on his way. I've been up for an hour and have already showered, was thinking about rousing the house out of its hungover stupor and start the after-party cleanup. My own head aches a bit from too much beer and my nose and sinuses feel fried from the coke, and the homophobic food smells fantastic.

He sits down on my bed and grins at me. His eyes are bloodshot and he hasn't showered, he stinks of sweat and sex and he has a UCSF baseball cap turned backward to cover up how messy his hair is. His lower face is covered with razor stubble. He hands me a large soda with condensation all over the cup, a wrapped hamburger, and a little box of fried zucchini. I pop one of the zucchinis in my mouth and it's perfect, hot and fried and tasting like breading and grease. He opens my nightstand drawer and pulls out my pipe, loads it and takes a hit without even asking but I'm too busy shoving food into my mouth to say anything. I didn't eat anything before the party and I'm starving.

He blows out the smoke and smiles at me. "Mission accomplished," he says.

I raise my eyebrows and swallow a mouthful of food. "Dylan?"

"No, but progress made on that front." He dumps French fries all over his burger wrapper. "Ricky." He frowns at the food. "You wanna hit the gym later? I'm gonna need to work off all this fat."

"Ricky? Do tell. And we're allowed a cheat day every week."

"Cheat day was last night with all that beer."

"Beer doesn't count."

He rubs his stomach. "Beer does count. I feel bloated."

I wave my hand. "Sure, I'll go later. So tell me about Ricky already." God, the food is amazing even if it is homophobic.

"Well, you were right about one thing. He definitely likes sex now that he's tried it." He grins at me, a blob of ketchup on his chin. "I fucked him, he fucked me, I taught him how to suck a cock properly." He wipes his chin with a napkin. "I really could teach a sex class."

"And he didn't feel guilty?"

"He didn't at the time. I'm sure when he wakes up today he's going to want to light a candle and say a novena." He laughs. "He's gorgeous, though, I will give him that. What about you? Any luck?"

I shake my head. "Kenny passed out in here around midnight. He was in a fine rage and was upset he couldn't find Ricky—thanks for solving that little mystery—so I got him nice and stoned and he passed out."

"You didn't take advantage of him?"

"Not my type." I put the last of the cheeseburger in my mouth and wash it down with a swig of Coke. I reach over and take the pipe from him, taking a hit. The residual nausea is gone thanks to the food, and I already feel better, but getting high never hurts. "Don't you want to know why Kenny was so upset?"

"Not really."

"Trust me, you want to know." I fill him in on the dynamic between Kenny and his sister, who just happens to be Dylan's best friend, and Brandon just laughs.

I hate when he does that.

"Yeah, Kenny's sister is a cock-blocker all right," and he tells me about how he sent Joey in after the one girl, and he could tell Dylan wasn't happy about how his best friend was acting, "so I'm getting closer and closer, and once Dylan is mine, you know what you have to do."

"Nothing, because you aren't going to fuck Dylan," I reply. I crumple up the wrappers and toss them into the bag. "Come on, now, we've got to get the house cleaned."

DYLAN Hangovers suck.

I don't even want to get out of bed. I just want to lie here until I die, which hopefully will be soon. I just want someone to come into my room and shoot me in the head.

Is that too much to ask? Apparently so.

I don't think I've ever been as drunk as I was last night. After the fight with Joni I kept drinking and wound up in someone's room whose name I can't remember playing drinking games until about three in the morning when I finally staggered out of there and up the stairs and somehow made it back to my room. I'm still wearing my clothes from last night and I can smell my armpits and my legs are sticky because someone spilled beer on me at some point and it seemed funny at the time and I need to get out of bed and shower but I'd rather just lie here and die.

Ugh, I'm going to have to deal with Joni fallout today, too.

Seriously, I wish someone would just come in and shoot me.

Then again, fuck her. Why is it my responsibility to make peace?

I don't need someone to guard my chastity.

It's *my* life.

And I don't need someone to tell me I shouldn't cheat on Marc.

The whole idea behind it is totally offensive. Because I'm not strong enough to resist some guy who wants to sleep with me? I'm too stupid to know when I'm being played?

THANK YOU JONI PLEASE PLEASE PLEASE TELL ME WHAT TO DO BECAUSE I'M TOO STUPID TO FIGURE IT OUT ON MY OWN.

I mean, really.

If I treated her the way she treats me…it's just a shame it took me this long to figure it all out.

We've always been close, ever since we were kids. We've always had fun together, but at some point as we got older, our friendship changed. I'll always be grateful to her for not caring that I was gay when I came out to her, but even now, thinking back on when I did, her response was kind of…

"Oh, I'm so glad you've finally accepted it!" was what she said. At the time, and ever since, I saw it as meaning she knew me better than I thought she did and she loved me so much that it didn't matter…but it shouldn't have mattered, should it?

Why was I grateful that me being gay didn't change anything?

Why was I grateful that my best friend was a decent human being?

My head hurts.

It's funny how conditioned we are to not see the systemic homophobia, to be grateful for the crumbs the straight people let us catch from the table we're still not allowed to sit at. If someone would have told me that just a week ago, I would have laughed at them and said my friends weren't homophobic, they were good allies...my best friend who doesn't think I'm smart enough to figure out my own life, who doesn't want me to have a boyfriend and fall in love and be happy...

I wonder if she would be so happy about me and Marc if he hadn't been shipping out.

Maybe I can write another essay for *Out* about this kind of thing.

Some of the comments on my essay about monogamy said that as gay men we shouldn't automatically default to the heteronormativity of monogamy and marriage; that we as gays and lesbians were actually in a position from the outside to come up with an entire new way of thinking about relationships that weren't tied to outmoded old religious models that actually came out of relationships as business contracts. At the time, I was defensive about my piece and my relationship.

Maybe I should go back and reread those comments, think about it some more.

My head hurts.

But it's worth thinking about, isn't it? And shouldn't I be grateful to Brandon for making me see things from a different perspective?

You just want to fuck Brandon.

"Go fuck yourself, Joni," I say out loud and reach for my phone where it sits on the windowsill to check it for emails and texts and things. I shut the ringer off at some point last night because I was tired of getting text messages from Joni, all of them angry, all of them nasty, and really, if I'm such an awful friend why does she want to be friends with me in the first place?

The message icon has the number 25 next to it.

Really?

Twenty-five texts.

Obsess much?

And I bet not one of them is an apology or anything reasonable, an "I'm sorry you feel that way and I'm sorry I reacted the way I did and can we at least talk about this" non-apology which would go a long way. I mean, I'm willing to sit down and listen to her, but I refuse to be bullied anymore.

I'm sorry I hurt her feelings, but I'm not sorry I finally stood up to her.

My head aching, I start scrolling through the messages:

I can't believe you would talk to me like that after everything we've been through

I've never been so hurt and betrayed in my life how could you do this to me

Stop ignoring my texts! You're a terrible person

You're such an asshole! Where are me and Madison supposed to sleep?

The rest were more of the same, how horrible I am and I should be ashamed of myself and what were she and Madison supposed to do and I need to come let them into my room and I'm an awful person and how dare I treat her that way after everything she's done for me...

Everything she's done for me.

I sit there, staring at the messages for a while.

If I'm so awful, why bother?

I start typing out a response—*no wonder your brother hates you*—but don't send it. Responding is the worst thing I can do, and I'll be damned if I'll sink down to her level.

Fuck her. Have a nice life, Joni. I wish you all the happiness you deserve.

Seriously.

I get out of bed carefully, trying not to move my aching head too much, and have to stop and sit back as a wave of nausea almost makes me throw up and I sit there breathing in slowly to try to get it under control, swearing I am never going to get drunk again, and just the thought of beer makes me gag and there's a red cup sitting there on my nightstand about half full of beer and I can smell it and I open the window and dump it out and close the window as the heat hits me in the face and I grab my bathroom caddy and stagger outside to the bathroom. The hallway reeks of stale weed and sour alcohol and sweat. Someone got sick in the bathroom and someone's in the shower and I almost throw up myself but I manage to wash my face and brush my teeth and get back to my room without anything bad happening.

I try to remember the rest of the party after my fight with Joni. She'd stormed off and I'd gone looking for Brandon, wasn't able to find him anywhere. I knocked on his door because I could see the light was on but he didn't answer, and that was how I wound up wandering around and getting involved in the drinking games.

Oh, God, never again. I think there may have been tequila shots involved.

I need to eat something.

I start to text Brandon but stop.

What am I doing? But he's the only person I know in the house besides Kenny, and I don't know Kenny that well, and Joni and Madison probably ended up sleeping in his room and he's never liked me that much and he won't exactly be happy they wound up in his room instead of mine and I just can't deal.

But maybe if Joni and I aren't friends anymore, maybe Kenny and I can be now.

I put on some clothes. No, I'm just going to walk over to Togo's by myself and get something to eat. I need to be alone, the last thing I need right now is to have to make conversation.

But I can't help wondering what happened to Brandon last night, where did he go?

Did he sleep with someone? Was he in his room and not alone and that's why he didn't answer when I knocked?

I know I shouldn't care but I do.

What does that say about me?

I put on my clothes and grab my keys and check my phone. It's about 50 percent charged, and I check for messages again and none of them are from Brandon. All of them are from Joni. I start to delete them but screen cap them all first in case I need reminding of why she needs to apologize to me for everything, and then they're all gone and I slip it into my pocket and then think about Facebook and pull it back out again and check his Facebook page, but there's nothing there, he hasn't updated it since before the party last night, and I walk down the back stairs and out into the parking lot and I see Joni's car is gone. I hope she and Madison made it back to LA safely.

I start walking.

Christ, it's hot out here. The house is silent and there are smashed and broken red cups all over the parking lot and all kinds of other trash and empty liquor bottles and someone got sick by the basketball hoop and I look away and head for the sidewalk and wish that I had a car here and remember I was supposed to ride back to LA with Joni to get my car and now that's out and maybe I'll take the train, I don't know, but I need to get my car and maybe my mother will come back up here and I wonder where Brandon was last night and my phone vibrates in my pocket and I pull it out to see if Brandon texted me and it's not, it's from my editor and—

I have feelings for Brandon.

It hits me. Joni was right. She was still a bitch, but that doesn't mean she wasn't right, even if wasn't any of her business.

I'm attracted to him, but it's more than that. I can deal with an attraction.

I have feelings for him.

I start walking again.

Why does everything have to be so complicated?

RICKY I feel—strange.

As the sun was coming up I woke up in Brandon's bed, with his arm around me and cuddled into his body. I didn't dream, but I thought when I opened my eyes that maybe the whole night had been a dream—but his big hand over my shoulder in my line of sight was evidence I hadn't imagined or dreamed it all. I was no longer a virgin. I had gotten drunk and smoked pot and had sex for hours.

His warm body felt amazing next to mine. I was on my side and my head was resting on his arm and his other arm was loosely draped over my chest, his torso pressed into my back. His dick was resting against my butt, limp.

Would I have done this if I hadn't been drunk? If I hadn't been stoned?

I slipped out from under his arm, couldn't find my underwear, pulled on my shorts and my T-shirt and grabbed my shoes and socks and slipped out in the gray light, worried I was going to run into someone in the hallway, someone was going to see me.

I've heard about walks of shame before, but never knew what it meant.

Now I do.

I managed to slip into my room not seen by anyone. I undressed, got a fresh pair of underwear and slipped it on, climbed into my bed and stared at the ceiling until I fell asleep again.

Now I am awake again and not sure what to think, what to do.

I feel like I've betrayed Kenny. Should I tell him?

Or would that just hurt him for no reason?

I remember Brandon's words to me last night about that, and I wonder if I believed him or if it was me not being in my right mind and wanting to give in to lust and fornication…it sounds so silly now, lust and fornication, fornication and lust.

My rosary glitters in the late morning sun on my nightstand. I start to reach for it but I stop.

Lust and fornication, drunkenness and intoxication.

The words seem so…so old-fashioned and out of touch to me now.

Have I sinned? Is God angry with me, disappointed with my fall from grace?

And yet it was inevitable. Once I left the seminary, after deciding to live my life honestly and openly (to everyone but my parents, no sense in lying to myself) as a gay man it was only a matter of time before I committed these sins. None of us are without sin. If the intent is just as big a sin as the act, I have been sinning for years.

Should I pray to the Holy Mother to intercede for me?

Should I go to confession?

Was it really a sin?

Confession without remorse is meaningless, the penance merely a formality, a ritual. I may fool the priest but I won't fool God.

I don't feel like I sinned. I didn't know it was possible to feel the way Brandon made me feel. Just remembering how he felt inside me, how it felt to be inside him, how he tasted, the feel of his body pressed against mine is making my dick hard again, even though it is sore and achy from everything it did last night.

Why would God make such pleasure possible and make it a sin?

I wish there were some priest I could speak to who wouldn't judge me, who would understand how I feel, who could discuss all of this with me instead of telling me I'm going to hell and I can never do any of these things again if I want to be right with God.

I am unrepentant and convinced now more than ever that leaving the priesthood behind was the right thing for me to do.

Maybe someday I will be called back to Mother Church, and I will be more understanding and compassionate, a better servant of God for having sinned.

But it's not a sin, it can't be a sin.

I touch the rosary, almost expecting it to burn my fingers, but the beads feel slightly warm from sitting in the sunlight.

I sit up in the bed. My head hurts, and although my body feel strangely worn, it feels right somehow, like this is how it's supposed to feel.

My balls hurt and my dick is sore and I'm not sure I will be able to walk normally when I get out of my bed, but it's right somehow.

This is right somehow.

I feel like people will know when they look at me, that I've changed and will never be the same person again, like Eve eating from the apple that was original sin.

I don't feel guilty for betraying Kenny. I know I should but I don't. I love Kenny, but this is different.

I am not the same person I was when I woke up yesterday.

I feel like I've finally become a man.

Brandon has made me a man.

I wrap my arms around myself and lick my lips. I know I should get up, take a shower, and maybe walk to the coffee shop, get a start on my day, on my new life. Because that's how I feel—maybe it's silly and childish, but I feel as though my life is different now, that I am a different person, that I am now, finally, an adult, and everything I do from here on out will be the pattern for the rest of my life, and what I do, like everything that happened before to me, the decisions made and how I felt about things, no longer matter. They all led me here to San Felice, where I was meant to meet Kenny and fall in love with him and be introduced to sex, to my own sexuality and sensuality, by Brandon.

The old me, the virgin I was, was ashamed of my desires, ashamed of my erections and attractions and desires and wants. My faith did that to me, drove who I was deep underground, wrapping who I am and my potential in shame and sin. I reject those teachings. I still love my faith, I still love my Lord, I still love God and the Holy Trinity and believe that is my only path to salvation, but I cannot believe that loving someone is sin, I cannot believe that enjoying the pleasures of the flesh condemns me to an eternity of hell and misery.

I cannot believe that a loving God would do this to His creation.

I get out of my bed and stand up. I slip out of my underwear, toss it into the laundry basket, and stand naked in front of the mirror. I'm not ashamed I left my underwear in Brandon's room, but for now I am looking at myself in the mirror. I don't look different, even if I feel different; my nipples are sore and sensitive and there are places on my chest that are purplish-yellow where he bit and sucked on my skin and it felt very good, but he left marks that I'll have to hide…but why do I have to hide them? Why be ashamed to let other people see that I was loved? I stand there, looking in the mirror into my bloodshot eyes, remembering that I drank and smoked weed for the first time—Sergio and Lupe both smoke weed, but I never had before last night, it was one of the things Brandon showed me to make me a man—and that's probably why my mouth tastes so sour and dry and my throat aches and my lungs are a bit sore. I need to eat something, my body needs nourishment, but first before I do anything I have to get clean, so I reach for my robe and drape it over my body, slip my feet into my rubber thongs, grab my things, and walk to the bathroom. I can hear the water, someone is showering already, and I push through the swinging saloon doors. The bathroom's stench almost knocks me down and turns my stomach, the stench of piss and shit and vomit and sour everything, but I breathe through my mouth and go around the half-wall to the communal shower, and someone I don't recognize has his back to me and his head under the steady spray of the water. He is tall and muscular and strong and his broad back is muscular but covered with angry red pimples, and I'm not used to this yet, this community of showers where everyone is exposed to anyone who walks in, not even in high school—at Sacred Heart there were stalls for us to have privacy—but I put my towel down and shake off my robe and turn on the water.

The hot water feels amazing slaking over my body, and I put my head underneath the showerhead, start rubbing the bar of soap over my chest, flinching slightly when I touch my aching nipples, laughing at myself as I shampoo my hair and turn around so my back is to the wall. The brother showering next to me is one I have met since I got here but I don't remember his name, it was just in passing and he smiles at me, he has a snub nose and a pointed chin and his eyes look glazed a bit and he asks me if I had a good time at the party and I say yes did you and he nods and makes a thrusting motion with his hips and I try not to look at his crotch and I turn my head back under the spray and he is stepping out and toweling off and I wonder if I am going to ever be able to look at another guy ever again without wondering what it would be like to be inside him...

And I wonder when I can be with Brandon again.

Kenny doesn't have to know.

KENNY "Can I sit with you?"

I look up from my phone to see Dylan Parrish, of all

people, with his tray and his sandwich and bag of chips and soft drink standing next to my table at Togo's, and I don't know what to say so I just nod and he sits down across from me and there's an awkward silence and I feel like I should say something but what do I say to someone who's always pretty much always pretended I don't exist?

"Did you have fun at the party?" he says without looking at me as he unwraps his sandwich—turkey and guacamole and sprouts of course, just like Joni would order, and I want to just get up and leave but I don't want to be rude.

"I did. How about you?"

"Joni and I had a fight."

Duh. Like I don't have a million text messages on my phone that I haven't bothered to read from her. "I figured."

"Did she sleep in your room last night?"

"Nope." No need for him to know I wasn't there. I can't believe I fell asleep in Phil's room and was really glad no one saw me sneaking out of there this morning even though nothing happened. People love to gossip and talk about people, and the last thing I need is for Ricky to find out I spent the night in Phil's room and I don't want to have to explain anything to him and I don't want to hurt him. "Where Joni slept isn't my problem. I didn't invite her up here." I don't add that this was the first time she's been up to San Felice since I started going to school here, so it's not like she came to see me in the first place.

"I didn't invite her either."

I look at him in surprise. That must have been a hell of a fight.

He tears open the bag of chips—barbecue Lay's, to be exact, the only greasy thing on his tray besides the soft drink, which is probably diet—and dumps them out on the tray. "Joni…" He pauses. "You know."

"No, I don't. You know her better than I do."

He flushes under his tan. "Look, we've never been friends, and I know that's probably my fault, and I get it, but we're both going to be here living in the same fraternity house and we're brothers and we should try now, don't you think?"

I think you want to be friends with me now because you've finally figured out what a total bitch my sister is, but okay. "Okay." They're going to make up anyway and that'll be the end of that, but it won't kill me to be nice to him. "Congratulations on your engagement, by the way."

"Thanks." He hesitates and asks, "Do you believe in monogamy?"

What? I just stare at him. "You're the expert, aren't you?"

He nods a bit. "I know, it's what me and Joni fought about, I don't know anymore. I love—" He stops. "I love Marc, I do, but…I'm having feelings for someone else now and I don't know if that's normal, and a straight girl won't understand and I don't have anyone else I can talk to—"

"And I'm the only gay guy you know?"

He nods.

"You know as well as I do I've never had a boyfriend." I don't want to talk to him about Ricky, I don't want Joni to know and I know he'll tell her all about it when they make up and they'll make fun of me and laugh at me the way they always have and I'm not entirely sure he's not setting me up right now but he looks like he means it. "So I don't know. I mean, if you love someone you're not supposed to be attracted to someone else, are you?"

"But that's just it," he replies. "That's what straight people do. And they all cheat on each other all the time! Their divorce rate is over fifty percent! More than half! So maybe they're doing it wrong?"

"Or are you just trying to justify cheating on your fiancé to yourself?"

"Maybe. Maybe I am. I don't know." He shakes his head,

slurps some soda up through the straw. "I am attracted to this other guy, but he's a nice guy, you know? I'd heard things about him before—"

"Are you talking about Brandon Benson?" I try not to laugh. It wouldn't be nice now that we're being all friendly, but seriously? Brandon Benson? Brandon is a dog who'll fuck anything that moves. "All he cares about is getting laid, you should know that, if you are talking about him, I mean."

"Are you sure?" He wants me to tell him Brandon's a nice guy, I can see it on his face, and it finally hits me that this is what he and Joni fought about, and I remember all the times they left me out of things, all the times they deliberately excluded me and made me the butt of their jokes and didn't invite me to things and wouldn't let me come along with them or wouldn't let me hang out with them at parties and everything, and now he's here at *my* school and *my* fraternity and he's fought with my sister and he's mad at her and he wants *me* to be his friend and tell him...

I take a drink from my own soda. I look him right in the eyes. "I know Brandon sleeps around a lot"—not a lie—"but he's always kind of struck me as...I don't know, like a nice guy who's been hurt? Like he doesn't want to get involved with someone because he doesn't want to get hurt again?" Okay, I can't believe I said that with a straight face.

And he believes me because he wants to believe me, oh, he's got it bad. For a moment I feel guilty, I think about his fiancé in the military and I think I should maybe be honest with him, but Joni was honest with him, and if he didn't want to hear it from his best friend he sure as hell doesn't want to hear it from me.

And besides, I don't owe him anything but payback, do I?

"That's what I think, too." My God, he's an idiot. You can't fix stupid. "I don't know what to do."

"Have you talked to your fiancé?"

"Marc? No, I haven't. Do you think I should?"

"Don't you owe it to him to be honest? If you really care?" "You're right." He smiles at me. "I do. Thanks, Kenny." "What are friends for?" I smile back at him. I can't believe he can't tell how much I hate him.

PHIL "Yes, yes, the party went extremely well, thank you. The new air-conditioning system is amazing, thank you for that," I say into my phone, rolling my eyes. "You did get the donation letter I sent you? Great. I'm so glad to hear that..."

Blah blah blah. I've got my head stuck so far up Rubin Monterro's ass I can see what he had for lunch. I can't wait till the day comes when I can tell him to go fuck himself. That day will come, but until then, as long as I am chapter president, I have to keep kissing his ass and humbling myself. I do enjoy listening to him talk about how much Ricky is enjoying being a Beta Kappa pledge and how welcoming all the brothers staying in the house have been to him since he arrived and how Rubin is especially pleased at the extra effort I've made.

If he knew Brandon was fucking his nephew's brains out pretty much every night, I don't know if he'd feel quite the same.

Maybe he would. I don't know. But given what a homophobe the old jackass is, I kind of doubt it.

Brandon has been having a great time turning Ricky into a greedy little slut. I have a ton of pictures on my phone of Ricky being fucked or sucked or being violated any number of ways. I'm sure Ricky has no idea Brandon's been taking pictures of him. Brandon is gorgeous, I'll give him that, and Ricky's really taken to the whole idea of getting laid. Since the Baby Bash party, he's pretty much insatiable, and I've been giving him advice.

That Monday after the party, he came to my room and told me everything. His conscience was bothering him, he told me, because Kenny has no idea what he'd been doing with

Brandon, and even though Brandon had told him he had nothing to be ashamed of, apparently all the Catholic brainwashing he's dealt with since he was in diapers was rearing its ugly head again and he just needed reassurance from someone who wasn't benefitting from his appreciation for whoring.

I rolled a joint and offered it to him, but he declined, saying that maybe pot was clouding his mind and his judgment.

"Ricky, you know I have only your best interests at heart," I somehow managed to say without laughing, "and I can see you're upset about something. I'm glad you feel comfortable talking to me."

That was all it took, he wouldn't stop talking and of course I knew all of it already, Brandon had told me all about everything they'd done and how much Brandon had liked it. I knew that Ricky was the one who came to Brandon's room the second time, knocking on his door like a cat in heat, and the second night was even more intense than the first and he couldn't blame the second night on being drunk, now could he? He didn't know what to do, he didn't feel right about having sex with Brandon while dating Kenny and it felt like he was cheating and yawn bore me to death you really do belong in a monastery blah blah blah and I managed to not slit my wrists in front of him or laugh at him but somehow kept an interested look on my face as I listened and wondered how he functioned in life.

"But if you and Kenny aren't"—inwardly I winced as I said the words—"going steady"—because we're in junior high school of course, maybe you should pass him a note in gym, Ricky dear—"I don't see how you can be cheating on him, or am I missing something?"

"No, we're not, we didn't talk about that, but—"

"Well, maybe you should talk to him about it." I cut him off. "Maybe Kenny isn't interested in being exclusive. You can't know that without asking him, now can you?"

He made an *O* with his mouth. "You're right."

I reached and patted his leg. "Do you want to stop doing what you're doing with Brandon?" How it nauseated me to be so delicate!

"No. No, I don't."

Little whore. "Then wait for Kenny to decide. I wouldn't bring it up if I were you. It's very simple."

"But isn't that kind of lying?"

Thank God I don't have a Catholic conscience.

"Ricky." I smiled at him. "Let me explain something to you about the real world. I know you were in a seminary, but out here in the real world there are shades of gray. You don't want to stop being with Brandon, and you enjoy seeing Kenny, right?" He nodded. "There's absolutely no reason for you to not do both for as long as you like."

"But—I'm not in love with Brandon."

"Sex and love aren't the same thing. You don't have to be in love with someone to have sex with them, you know. You can just have sex for the sake of having sex." I gestured broadly around the room. "I don't want a boyfriend until I get out of school. I don't have the time to devote to one, you know? Between school and studying and running the house and being a good brother, it wouldn't be fair for me to be involved with someone. But that doesn't mean I don't have needs and urges." I closed my eyes and tilted my head. "And sometimes watching porn on the internet just isn't enough."

"Oh my God, no, it's not, I mean, now that I know what—" He stopped himself.

"Ricky. It's okay to watch porn, it's okay to—you know, masturbate to it." Talking to him is like talking to a child. What on earth kind of parents did he have? "But sometimes it's nice to be with an actual human being. You were raised to believe that being gay was a sin—that's what your church actually believes—and that even just thinking about it is as bad as doing it. So why not just do it?" I shrugged. "I mean, if you're going to burn…"

I practically saw the lightbulb come on over his head. "Yes, that makes sense."

"And as for Kenny…you like him, don't you?"

He nodded.

"But you're not sleeping with him?" God, the euphemisms.

He shook his head.

"Then have fun with Brandon. When you and Kenny get to that point, then worry about whether you want to have two lovers or just one. But there's nothing wrong with what you're doing. Nothing. And don't let anyone ever make you think that again."

He left me alone then, and he's been Brandon's regular fucktoy every night since.

I don't know how Brandon stands it, to be honest.

Better him than me.

DYLAN I'm a coward.

I know I have to talk to Marc about these feelings I have for Brandon, but I can't do it. I can't bring myself to say the words to him. He knows something is up, though, because I'm not myself when we FaceTime. I tell him that it's hard for me to adjust being in San Felice rather than LA, and that I'm getting to know my new brothers and I'm still upset about the fight with Joni, but I can't tell him what the fight was about and he thinks it's silly that I won't just call her, but I just tell him she was awful and possessive and nasty to me and until she apologizes I am not willing to talk to her and I mean it and it's true, I don't miss her at all. It's kind of been a relief, honestly.

I had no idea how much of my free time she took up.

And who knew that her brother Kenny was such a great guy? Ever since I ran into him at Togo's the day after the party we've hung out a couple of times, and he's nothing like Joni made him out to be. He's actually nice and cool and funny and has a great sense of humor and I can't believe how rude and nasty she always was to him. I feel like I should apologize to him all the time, but whenever I try, he just dismisses it and tells me not to be stupid, it's life and it's in the past and not to worry about it anymore, we're friends now and that's all that matters.

And his boyfriend Ricky! What a sweet guy. They are so cute together. Ricky's actually one of the most gorgeous guys I've even seen in real life, I mean seriously he is model good looking, like if Mario Lopez and Nick Jonas somehow had a son that would be Ricky, and he has absolutely no idea of how good looking he is. He'd be King of Fire Island, that's for sure, and people are always stopping in their tracks whenever they see him and he has no clue, he's just a nice guy. So weird that he was going to be a priest, but he and Kenny are so sweet together that I like to just watch them together, how they interact, and seeing them makes me miss Marc, but at the same time I keep lying to him and how can I lie to him when I love him—what kind of love is that?

And Brandon. I can't stop thinking about Brandon.

Joni was so wrong about him.

We spend a lot of time together, me and Brandon, and we go to the grocery store to get supplies or to the mall to just hang out or to get something to eat or to see a movie or just down to the beach to get some sun and watch the surfers and he never tries anything, never touches me, never does anything other than be a perfect gentleman to me. Just being around him makes me happy, and I don't feel like I'm doing anything wrong…but we aren't doing anything other than being friends and hanging out together. I know, I know I think about him in ways I shouldn't. I want him to touch me, I want him to try something but am glad he doesn't because I wouldn't be able to say no to him. The way his tanned skin shines when the sun's on it and he's oiled up on the beach, the way his eyes twinkle when he smiles, the shy smile he gets when he's teasing me, the way he laughs when we're together...I have a picture on my phone that I took of him on the beach that...that captures his essence, who he is, he's wet and got goose bumps from being in the water and he's laughing and his dimples are deep and his eyes are glowing and the sun is shining on his muscles and he's oiled up so the water is beading up on him and I downloaded it to my computer, and sometimes before I go to bed...I pull it up on my computer and imagine what his body would feel like pressed up against mine, wonder what it would be like to have him on top of me and inside me and I can't help myself, I beat off thinking about it while I look at his picture and then I'm finished and I feel ashamed of myself, like I'm some kind of sick stalker or something.

One day I walked into the bathroom downstairs while he was showering and I swear it wasn't on purpose, I didn't know he'd be in there and I watched him shower for a full minute. His back was to me and his ass was so white and round and firm and the tan line was so clearly defined from the dark tanned skin and then he started to turn around and I had to duck into one of the bathroom stalls because I didn't want him to catch me watching him and I didn't want to see him nude from the front because I knew I wouldn't be able to stop thinking about him I can't stop thinking about him as it is and I know I have to tell Marc I can't keep this from him and what is wrong with me I have a great guy who loves me and wants to marry me and all I can do is think about Brandon...

BRANDON Joey is coming out of Phil's room as I walk up the hall and he smiles at me and says hey and salutes me and he isn't wearing a shirt and I can see his dick is still kind of hard inside his board shorts and there's a wet spot that's probably cum leaking out of him and I don't understand why Phil demeans himself the way he does sucking off these straight boys who would kick the shit out of him before they'd ever admit they love having him suck them off.

I know he's right, we would have never made it as a couple, one of us would have cheated on the other and then we would have started cheating to punish each other and it would have gotten ugly and we would have ended up hating each other in the end, but sometimes...sometimes I think it might not have gone that way, it didn't have to, and I realize I'm kind of jealous of Joey.

It surprises me so much I stop with my hand poised to knock on the door and think about it for a minute.

Should I say something to him about it?

No, he would laugh at me and never let me hear the end of it.

He's such a bitch.

But that's also why we get along so well.

I knock, and the door opens almost immediately and Phil smiles at me.

I reach up and wipe at the side of his mouth. "You missed some of Joey there."

"You're such a bitch." He steps aside and I walk past him through the office into his room. He shuts the door behind us and flops down on the bed. "If you want a joint, go ahead and roll one. Although I don't know why you never bring me weed anymore."

I shrug. "You come to my room, I'll get you high."

"As rarely as you change your sheets?" He laughs as I start rolling a joint. "Your bed is a petri dish of STDs."

"And you say I'm a bitch?" I light the joint and take a big hit. I hold it in as long as I can before blowing it out, feeling a nice mellow taking over my head. "You need to stop sucking straight dick. It's making you bitter."

He takes the joint from me and takes a hit. "I don't have time, he's convenient and undemanding." He hands it back. "I spoke to Rubin today—he thanked me for how welcome we've made Ricky feel since he got here." He smirks. "I thought it best not to tell him how whipped his nephew is."

I take another hit and grind the joint out. "He's kind of a good kid, you know?"

Phil opens his eyes wide in mock shock. "Is that a conscience you're growing there? Who are you and what have you done with Brandon?" He starts laughing.

"I didn't say I felt bad for him, I said he's kind of a good kid," I reply. I hate when he laughs at me, but saying something about it will just make him laugh harder. He really is a hateful bitch when he wants to be, and there's nothing he loves more than sensing weakness in someone else. "I don't know what the end game with Ricky is."

He shrugs. "No end game. I just thought it would be fun, you know…innocence perverted and all that. It makes dealing with Rubin and his bullshit so much easier for me, knowing that his precious nephew the ex-priest has turned into such a thirsty cock-slut."

I know I should be agreeing with him, laughing with him, but it doesn't seem funny to me anymore.

What's wrong with me?

"How is Operation Dylan coming along?" He raises an eyebrow. "Any progress?"

"It's just a matter of time," I say. I'm confident. I know Dylan has feelings for me, and they bother him. And now that his bitch friend Joni is completely out of the picture—well, there's no one telling him I'm bad news. He mentioned this afternoon at the beach he was thinking about writing another piece for *Out*, this time directly addressing people who criticized the monogamy piece and talking about how maybe monogamy isn't for everyone and really, whatever works best for the couple is what's right for them, and it was all I could do not to pump my fists in triumph, because whether he admits it or not, I am changing his mind about everything he believed, his values, because he was all about monogamy when we met on Fire Island and now he's not so sure.

But…for some reason, the victory feels kind of…hollow.

"You're not going to fuck that boy." He laughs again. "You may think you are, but you aren't going to. He's in love with his soldier boy, and it would make him the biggest hypocrite on the planet."

I clench my teeth. "I am going to fuck him, and once I do, I am claiming my prize."

He makes a face. "Your prize?"

"You bet me I wouldn't be able to, remember?"

He rolls his eyes. "Oh yes, of course, and when you do you get to spend the night with me." He laughs again. "Well, I won't hold my breath waiting for that to happen."

"You need to be fucked hard by someone who knows what they're doing."

He starts laughing again. "And that would be you?"

I get up. "You wait and see."

His laughter follows me out the door. I'm furious.

Oh yes, you little bitch. I'm going to fuck Dylan and then I am going to put you through your headboard.

No one laughs at me.

RICKY There's no one in the hallway when I reach up and knock on Brandon's door.

It's almost midnight and Kenny has gone to bed. We went out to dinner at a Mexican place down near the beach and then to a superhero movie, Kenny really loves those, he has boxes of comic books in his room's closet, wrapped in Mylar with cardboard backing, and he also downloads tons of them on his iPad, I don't think I've ever met anyone so into comic books before, but his enthusiasm is catching and I'm learning about them, the history of the superheroes and the artists and writers and the companies that make them. I think the movie was entertaining enough, but there wasn't much of a plot—well, what little there was didn't make sense, and most of it was just an excuse for fight scenes and explosions—but the main actor was gorgeous and he was shirtless or in a skintight outfit most of the time, and I have to admit he was very sexy.

Brandon opens the door and smiles at me. "I was wondering if you were coming by tonight or not."

"We went to a movie and we had to talk about it a bit before I could get away," I say as I step inside and he closes the door behind me. I reach down and grab him. He's already hard in his underwear and I want him inside me, I want him to fuck me deep and hard, and I press my lips against his and his tongue darts inside my mouth and I massage his dick with my right hand while I grab his ass with my left, the index finger probing inside the crack of his ass through the underwear the way he showed me and he grins at me and pushes me back toward the bed and I take off my shirt and throw it aside and slip down my shorts and I am naked under them, when I know I am coming down to Brandon's room I don't wear underwear and I know he still has that pair I left behind the first time I was with him in one of his drawers and that gives me a kind of secret thrill and there's only a small part of me that still thinks this is wrong and unfair to Kenny but my desire is so much stronger than that voice there's no need for me to even listen to it anymore, I don't care and Kenny has never brought up anything about being serious and exclusive and we still only kiss and I think it's kind of sweet. I asked him about doing more than kissing once and he told me he was a virgin and he wanted to take it slow because it meant something to him, and I wanted to tell him he was wrong, that it can be fun and amazing and you don't have to love someone to have sex with them, that was just puritanical church talk, but Dylan believes that too he even writes about it, but he seems to be changing his mind, too, and I moan as Brandon takes me in his mouth and I don't think about anything anymore...

DYLAN "What?" Marc is asking me from half the world away, a shocked look on his face, and my heart plummets and I wonder if I've lost him forever.

"Do you love him?" He looks bewildered, and sad, and my heart is breaking and I wonder how I could be doing this to him.

But what kind of relationship would we have if it wasn't based in honesty?

Not telling him would be lying, too.

"I don't love him," I reply. "I know that, but I do feel something for him, Marc. I don't know what it is...it's not like what I feel for you but there's something there. Maybe it's just attraction, I don't know. Oh, maybe I shouldn't have said anything. I'm so sorry."

"Give me a second, okay?" He gets up and walks away from the computer. All I can see is the tent wall behind him, and I again wonder what kind of a monster tells his fiancé in the military putting his life on the line for his country in a war zone on the other side of the planet that he might have feelings for another man.

And Joni said Brandon was an awful person. I am the awful person.

She was right about me.

I don't deserve friends I don't deserve Marc I don't deserve anything good in life.

I want to get drunk.

I want to get stoned.

I want to do something anything that will help me forget what a horrible piece of shit I am.

Marc sits back down in front of the laptop camera and gives me a weak smile. He doesn't look happy. I want to say something but I can't. I feel like he should tell me how he feels before I do anything, before I apologize, before I beg him to forget I said anything and I'll do anything to make it up to him and will spend the rest of my life—

"I can't say I'm happy about this," he says.

Oh shit.

"But I have a lot of time over here to think," he says, so slowly, like it's hurting him to talk and I feel like even more of an asshole, "and you know, it may surprise you, but I've actually thought about this before a few times, and you know what, I don't care."

WHAT?

He laughs. "You should see your face."

"I don't—I don't understand. You're not mad?"

He exhales loudly, and there's feedback for a moment and I wince. "No, I'm not mad, Dylan. I do love you and I want to marry you and have the house with the two kids and the dog and the picket fence and to live happily ever after, but I'm halfway around the world and I'm going to be gone for a long time, and you get lonely just like I get lonely, and I'm not going to throw everything we have together away just because you get lonely and meet some guy you like." He takes a deep breath and goes on. "And I love you and I want you to be happy. I don't want you to be miserable or sad or lonely. And if you meet someone—at any point in our lives, even after we're married—that you love more than you love me or you think will make you happier than I can make you, then I want you to be with that person. I don't want you to be with me because you feel obligated or something, you know?" He wipes at his eyes. "All I want is for you to be honest with me and know that you can always be honest with me because that's what love is all about, you know?"

I stare at his face, not able to say anything because I can't believe what I've heard, and I love him so much more in that moment it feels like my heart might explode in my chest.

"I love you so much," I hear myself saying.

"And I love you." He smiles at the camera. "Look, babe, I have to go. But it's okay, you know that?"

I nod.

"I love you."

"I love you."

The screen of my laptop goes black, and I close it. I lean back in my chair, unable to believe how lucky I am to have someone so kind and loving and understanding to love me the way he does, to put my own happiness before his own the way he just did, and—

Wait a minute, he said that he gets lonely, too.

No, don't be silly. That didn't mean anything, that's the kind of thing Joni would say to you, make you doubt him, to cause trouble and—

Maybe the reason he's being so understanding is because maybe there's someone in his unit…

Stop that right now.

He would tell me, wouldn't he? He said that as long as we were honest with each other—

I'm projecting, that's all this is.

I should be working on my new op-ed, but I can't focus. I get up and look at the clock. Eight thirty. I pick up my iPhone and there's no texts, no messages. I told Brandon I had to talk to Marc and then I was going to work on my op-ed, so I wasn't free to do anything tonight.

It would be shitty of me to see if he didn't have plans, wouldn't it?

But I want to talk to him, and it's not like I expect him to break any plans he might have made.

I start typing out a text to him but delete it instead of hitting send.

I've got to—I know, I'll just go get a soda from the machine in the lobby. I scrounge up some quarters and head down the hallway and down the stairs. The house is deserted and weirdly quiet, no one's in the lobby and no one's in the big room and the television is off and there's no music coming from anywhere and it's weird, I'm not sure, and for a minute I think *oh this is like one of those zombie movies where the hero suddenly realizes there's no one else alive or a scary movie where the maniac with a knife is waiting just around the corner* and I laugh and put the quarters in and hit the button for Diet Coke and the machine makes its clunky noise and the can pops out at the bottom in the slot. I pick it up and head back for the stairs, and just as I go around the corner, the door to the office opens and I almost jump out of my skin.

"Whoa! Didn't mean to scare you!" Phil says, and he's not wearing a shirt and his shorts are hanging down low and I can see his plaid boxers in the dim light coming from behind him in the office. I can vaguely smell pot and I hesitate for just a minute, but if I'm out of line I don't care.

"Do you have any—" I stop and shake my head.

"Any what?" He smiles back at me and tilts his head to one side, and I've never noticed before how nice looking he is. He's not blow-your-mind hot like Brandon is, and he's in good shape but not overly muscled—he's more toned than anything else—and the way the light is coming from behind him, it makes his blond hair glow like a halo.

Why not?

"I was wondering if I could talk to you, if you had a minute?"

"Sure." He smiles, and he has perfect teeth because of course he does, everything about him is perfect and I feel insecure, awkward, ugly, and stupid and it's overwhelming and he gestures for me to go inside and says, "I just need to run get a soda," and I feel a bit of relief because he drinks soda, too, so he won't judge me. I walk into his room, the presidential suite, and it's nice.

The president's room at our chapter at UCLA wasn't

nearly as nice as this one, which is about twice as big and has a private bathroom. The door is open and I can see it's got a huge shower with one of those waterfall spigots in the roof and it's glass, and he's got posters up of beautiful places like the pyramids at sunset and the Parthenon at night, and there's also some movie posters, *Thor* and *Guardians of the Galaxy*. I sit down in a chair near the bed and I can see there's some roaches in the ceramic ashtray on his nightstand, and it does smell a lot like pot in here and I wonder if he'll offer me some because I really need to relax, and maybe I'll just be forward and ask and the worst thing he can do is say no and think I'm an asshole, and I don't care, I really don't care I know he and Brandon are close but I want to ask him his opinion.

He comes back in, shuts the door behind him, sits down on the bed, and opens his Coke—regular, not diet or caffeine free—and he smiles at me and says, "I allow myself one of these a day, they're really terrible for you and I shouldn't even have the one, but it's kind of a treat for me even if it's murder on my waistline," and I just kind of laugh in response and say he has nothing to worry about on that score, he could probably have a six-pack a day, and as soon as I say it I'm mortified and I can't believe I said it and could bite my tongue off and just want to run and hide in my room.

"You're very sweet," he says, taking a drink and then burping and laughing again, "sorry, but the burp is sometimes the best part," and I start laughing with him but he's relaxed and I'm laughing nervously and being stupid and idiotic and I wonder if the floor would just do me a favor and open up a big hole to swallow me whole.

"I've not really done a very good job of welcoming you," he is saying now, "but you got here right before the Baby Bash, and I've been trying to get the budget for the new semester until control and I have a paper to write for a class I'm taking this summer, but that's really not an excuse."

And I smile and tell him it's no big deal, I've been settling in just fine, which is true, and I look over at the ashtray.

He reaches over and retrieves the biggest roach, it's half a joint, and he says, "Do you?"

I nod and he lights it and hands it to me and I take a nice hit and hold the smoke in. It's very good stuff, I should have known he'd have the best, and I don't know what to say and I blow out the smoke and say, "I need some advice, do you mind? I just need someone, you know, to talk to."

"Of course, that's what I'm here for, I'm always available. What's going on? Is there something I can do to help you?"

And I take another hit and everything is pouring out of me, how I feel about Brandon and how bad I feel about betraying Marc and then talking to Marc on the phone and how Marc reacted and I'm not sure how to feel about that and I don't know what I should do, and he raises an eyebrow and listens, and he really is listening, he's looking deep in my eyes and listening and it's so nice to actually have someone really listen and now I understand why he got elected president because if he listens to everyone like this, really pays attention to people, that's a rare quality and it makes me feel special, makes me feel like he cares and I keep talking, blabbing on and on and take another hit from the joint and then he stubs it out and I am stoned, really stoned, and it feels good and I sit back and wait for him to say something.

"Brandon is my friend," he says carefully, "and we've been friends ever since he transferred here. He's a great guy, he's a lot of fun and I care about him a lot, but I would be lying if I said he was the kind of guy anyone would want to try to have a relationship with, to fall in love with. Brandon's a heartbreaker. He's left a trail of broken hearts in his path." He shakes his head. "I hate to tell you that, and it makes me feel like a bad friend to him, but I have to be honest with you. I think it would be a mistake for you to get involved with him."

"We're just friends," I say, knowing it's a lie as soon as I say it, and just the act of saying it out loud and knowing it for the lie it is makes me understand who I am a bit more, and I know I have been lying to myself ever since I first laid eyes on Brandon next to the pool at Jordy's house on Fire Island. I knew as soon as I saw him he was dangerous, he was too good looking and I wanted him and deep inside my heart I was sorry I hadn't met him before getting engaged to Marc.

"It doesn't sound like you're just friends."

"I don't know what we are," I say, and it's true. I don't know what to do. "I like him a lot, I do, but I'm engaged to someone and I love Marc and..." I stop talking and feel like an idiot, can't believe I've said all of this to someone I barely know, but he's my fraternity brother and that counts for something, and I had to talk to someone but am glad I don't have Joni anymore because she would just be a *bitch*.

"If you love Marc, do you really want to take that risk?"

"But I told Marc. I told him because I don't ever want to keep secrets from him and I know it was maybe not the kindest thing to do but if I can't be honest with him"—I know I'm babbling, but the pot is making me think that I'm not being clear and honest with him and he needs to understand, I've got to make him understand—"then we're not really meant to be. I should be able to tell him anything, right? And he said he understood and he just wanted me to be happy and we can't be together right now and he doesn't want me to feel like I can't be honest with him and he understands everything and it makes me feel like I'm an even worse person than I thought I was before and I just don't know what to do."

"I can't tell you what to do, you know," he says finally, after an agonizing moment where I wish I were dead and had never run into him in the first place. "Only you can decide what you want to do, what's worth taking a risk for. If I were you, I'd be grateful I had someone like Marc—I mean, what a great guy, who loves you and trusts you enough to say it's okay for you to have feelings for another man? He's one in a million. That alone would give me the strength to be firm with Brandon, to only be friends. He's a good friend," he stops and thinks for a moment, "but the reason we are such good friends is because I would never for a second consider being anything other than his friend." He shivers a little bit. "Maybe he does care for you, Dylan. Maybe you're the one who's different." He shrugs. "But every single one of the other guys before you thought that, too."

PHIL That shakes him up a little bit. He goes pale and he swallows, can't even look me in the eye, looking around the room.

Such a fucking idiot on every level. I should let Brandon go ahead and fuck some sense into him. I shouldn't have said anything at all. I should have just let him go on thinking he's special and that Brandon honestly has feelings for him and blown it all. He deserves it, after writing that stupid, offensive, homophobic anti-sex piece in the first place. He deserves to be outed to the entire world as a hypocrite and a phony and everything else that would happen to him, being laughed at and talked about and mocked.

He deserves every little bit of it.

But I'm not going to wrap him up and put a ribbon on him and deliver him to Brandon.

Brandon needs to work for this one.

And this little idiot is so beneath Brandon. Really.

I want to just grab him by the shoulders and shake him.

He's wearing a goddamned engagement ring, he's promised to marry someone, and now he is going to let Brandon mess that up for him?

I should tell him the truth, that all he is to Brandon is another notch in his belt and he thinks it's funny to get the poster boy for gay monogamy.

But of course, I can't. I can't tell him now without making

myself look like a complete asshole, and if I'm going to run this place and turn it into the fraternity it should be, all the brothers—every single one of them—has to think, has to believe, that I'm a great guy, a good brother, the standard bearer of the ideals of Beta Kappa.

All of which, I might add, is a fucking crock in the first place. They all pay lip service, but being a brother in this house isn't like having eighty best friends. The brothers are no different than any other group of people. They're petty and backstabbing and two-faced, and none of them can be trusted not to knife you in the back if given the chance.

I mean, seriously. If Beta Kappa was real, if we all actually lived up to our creed and our ideals and our standards, would Brandon be trying to fuck with this kid? No, he wouldn't. And Brandon is no different than anyone else in this house.

The only reason I've gotten to be president—and made everyone in the house feel like I'm the fucking living incarnation of Beta Kappa—is because I'm better at playing the game than the rest of them. I'm too smart to get caught.

The only person who knows the real me is Brandon—and he'd never say anything because he's not able to; he'd go down with me.

Mutually assured destruction.

So instead of telling this idiot the fucking truth and slapping some sense into him, I have to sit here and try to convince him that sleeping with Brandon isn't in his own best interests.

If it weren't so sad it would be comical.

I mean, seriously. Could this kid be any bigger of an idiot?

Brandon doesn't have feelings for him. Brandon doesn't have feelings for anyone besides Brandon.

If he was going to fall in love with anyone, it would have been *me*.

And he didn't fall in love with me. He didn't commit to me.

There's absolutely no way he could possibly have feelings for this prim little—smug little—I absolutely refuse to believe it no matter how much Dylan Parrish wants to believe it.

I should be enjoying this more, after reading that fucking op-ed he wrote about monogamy, about how sad and pathetic promiscuous gay men are, how he would never be one of those men—you could practically read the scorn dripping from his words, the sneer on his face as he typed them, believing them all, smug and prim and proper and virginal with his engagement ring on his finger and his fiancé serving.

The picture of him that ran with the piece was bad enough. I wanted to slap the smug superior smile right off his face.

And now Brandon's got him rethinking it all, wondering if monogamy is everything he thought it was, wanting to drop his drawers and bend over and take it right up the ass and be Brandon's little bitch boy.

But if he does, Brandon will be insufferable. And it's past time for Brandon to be brought down a couple of notches.

I mean, look how long it took him to do me the favor I asked him for! I practically had to beg him, and look at Ricky! LOOK AT HIM.

Compared to this mealy-mouthed little douchebag?

No, I won't have it.

You will not have Brandon, and Brandon won't have you.

Not if I can help it, bitch.

DYLAN He lights another one of the roaches and hands it to me.

I'm so confused.

I don't know what to do, what I'm thinking.

This is some seriously good weed, though, I am getting so high and feeling a lot more relaxed than I did when I came in here. Phil's a good guy, and I'm glad I transferred here, I'm glad I have a president and a brother like Phil to turn to, to confide in and talk to.

"Believe me," Phil says, looking me right in the eyes, "I want to believe Brandon's changed, can care about someone else. I've just seen it happen so many times before. He might be interested at first, but he gets bored and moves on. I've seen so many hearts get broken by him. And you—you have so much more than any of those other guys had to lose, Dylan! I mean, your monogamy piece was so important and so heartfelt—" He breaks off.

"Thanks," I reply. Wow, I am so high, my head feels like it weighs a hundred pounds. "I meant it at the time I wrote it, but now I'm not so sure. I mean, maybe men aren't supposed to be monogamous, with the whole propagation of the species thing, you know, how men are biologically engineered to spread their seed everywhere—"

"Don't be silly," he says. "When I fall in love I want to be in love, I want the man I love to love me and only me—"

"But sex isn't love."

He stares at me, blinking, his mouth open in a round *O* of shock. "That sounds like something Brandon would say," he says quietly, so softly I almost can barely hear it, and he shakes his head. "You've got it bad, Dylan. You might need to go away for a while, clear your head."

"What do you mean?"

"You aren't taking any summer classes, are you? Go home. Go spend some time with your parents. Get out of San Felice before you do something you're going to spend the rest of your life regretting."

"Maybe—maybe you're right." I stand up and almost lose my balance. I am so stoned. I pick up my soda can and say thanks to him and mean it, and I smile and say I'm going to go up to my room and lie down and think about it for a while, and I hear him close the door behind me and I go back up the stairs and almost lose my balance more than once and I make it to the top of the stairs and there's someone upstairs in the dark hallway and I hope he doesn't notice how high I am there's nothing like making an impression on someone you barely know by being so fucked up you can barely walk and I'm trying not to weave as I head for my room reaching into my pocket for my room key maybe he's right maybe I need to go visit my parents get away for a little while get my head back together Brandon is all wrong for me it would be a mistake to have feelings for him I love Marc dammit I want to spend the rest of my life with Marc—

"Dylan?" he says and I turn around and he's standing there with a bemused look on his face, he's not wearing a shirt because of course he never wears a shirt, and he takes my key and unlocks my door and opens it and I stumble inside and he closes it behind me and says with a bit of a laugh, "You're high, aren't you?"

"What if what if I am?" I am swaying, I know I am and I know he is laughing at me, but fuck it, I don't care. "Ever since I met you I've been off balance." I hiccup and almost spill my Diet Coke, but Brandon snatches it out of my hand and pushes me gently so I sit down on the bed hard.

"Lie down and sleep it off," he says, kissing the top of my head.

I sit back up. "I don't want to sleep it off, and yes, I am really high and it's your fault."

"My fault?" He's just standing there, looking at me, smiling that infuriatingly sexy smile, his shorts riding low enough for me to tell he's not got any underwear on, and I want him, I do want him, damn it all to hell, I do want him.

I don't know what to say I don't know what to tell him, because I can't say what I want to say, I'm so fucking high and that was a mistake, I can't handle him when I'm this messed up and I lie back on the bed and put my head on the pillows and fold my arms and he sits down at the foot of my bed by my feet and is still smiling at me.

"How is you being this high my fault?"

"Oh, you know why," I finally say, and that has to be good enough because I'm not going to say anything else. I can't tell him how I feel. I can't tell him how much I want to kiss him and feel his arms around me and...and...and he says, "What's this?" and he looks at my desk and my laptop is open and the picture, oh my God the picture of him at the beach is open and he looks back at me.

"Why do you have this picture of me on your laptop?" He's smirking at me, he knows the answer but he wants me to say it, he's going to make me say it, well FUCK YOU BRANDON BENSON I'm not going to say it.

"It's a nice picture." My words seem slurred to me. "I like looking at it, I did a good job."

"It is a good picture, can you send it to me?" He's smiling back at me now, closes my laptop so the picture is gone from view. "I want to make it my profile pic on Facebook."

"Uh-huh," I say and I am so relaxed now, my eyelids are heavy I AM TOO HIGH and I can't stop it, I'm drifting off and as humiliating as it is I can't stop it, I can't...

BRANDON He's snoring a little bit, poor little stoned boy.

It won't hurt to lie down and cuddle with him a little bit, will it?

Ricky won't be showing up at my door for hours, anyway.

DYLAN I wake up and the clock on my nightstand says eleven and my stomach is growling and I realize I'm not alone in my bed, I'm lying on my side with my back to someone and there's an arm draped over me, and in that moment I know that it's not Marc and then it flashes through my mind what happened before I fell asleep and I know it's Brandon.

Brandon is in bed with me. I passed out in front of him and he got into my bed with me.

I don't know what to do.

Should I feel violated? But my shirt and my shorts are still on, and he's asleep, I can tell by his even breathing, and his chest is against my back and I can feel his breath on the back of my neck and it's actually more sweet than anything else.

Sweet. Brandon is being sweet.

He could have done anything he wanted to me. I was so high and wasted I wouldn't have been able to say no to anything he wanted, even if I wanted to say no, but I wouldn't have. He could have taken total advantage of me and he didn't.

I'm not totally sober even now, but he feels so warm, his body feels so lovely against mine—even better than those times when Marc and I have spent the night together—I don't want to wake him up. But I'm thirsty and there's no way I can drink my Diet Coke lying down.

And if I do sit up, and then curl back up with him again...

That would be admitting it.

Friends can cuddle, but I don't think of him as a friend anymore.

I love him.

Not the same way I love Marc, but I do love him. I'm attracted to him, I want to be with him, and I want him inside me and I want to love him, I want to explore his beautiful body with my hands and my mouth and my tongue, I want to do things with him I never thought about doing with Marc or having Marc do to me, and maybe that makes me a slut and a hypocrite, but I don't care.

I gently move his arm off me and sit up carefully, so carefully, trying not to disturb him or wake him up. The Diet Coke is lukewarm and going flat but I take a big sip from it,

WICKED FRAT BOY WAYS

muffle the inevitable belch and wonder if I can lie back down and move his arm back in place when I realize his eyes are open and he's watching me.

He smiles when he knows I know he is awake and he says, "I just like watching you."

And my heart melts and I lie back down, facing him this time, our noses very close, looking deep into his eyes and losing myself in them, and I know he won't make the first move, I'm going to have to do it, so I move closer to him and press my lips against his. He doesn't kiss me back at first. For a brief second I'm terrified that I've done the wrong thing, but then he pressed back against me, slips his arms around me, and pulls me in closer, and he tastes like toothpaste and his heart is pounding deep inside his chest, I can feel it through his hot skin and we keep kissing gently, it's very sweet and kind and loving, and I like it, even though I want to let everything go and become one with him.

He pulls his head back and whispers, "Are you sure you want to do this, Dylan?"

I open my mouth but nothing comes out, so I nod and my heart is racing with an excitement I've never felt with Marc, and I wonder if I truly love Marc or if I just love the idea of Marc—

Stop that! Don't think that! That's wrong!

—but being with him here and now feels the way I've always thought it should feel, when I was a virgin and trying to come to terms with my own sexuality and the crushes I was developing on the boys in gym class, stealing looks at them in the shower, dreaming of the day when someone would make me feel the way the Beast made Belle feel, the way Jasmine made Aladdin feel, and Ariel and Eric and all the other couples in my wonderful Disney movies, and I used to dream of the day my prince would come for me, and I thought it was Marc but this is different, this is so much better and different than

Marc, and I'm overwhelmed and my eyes fill with tears and I don't want him to see me cry.

"We don't have to do anything," he's barely speaking, the words are like breaths, "I love you too much to want to ever do anything you'd regret."

And I kiss him as hard as I can, press my hips forward and no matter what he might be saying I can tell he is aroused, he wants me as much as I want him, and I say, "Brandon, I am in my right mind and I want you so much. I love you, Brandon. I do."

And then he's rolling me up on top of him and he is kissing me, and I know he is going to be inside me soon and I'm happier than I've ever been in my life, I've loved and wanted him from the very first and I am so glad, so glad that he wants me back and he loves me, he does, everyone was wrong about him, he loves me, and my shorts and my shirt are gone, taken off somehow and thrown aside and his shorts are down and he is inside me, he's so big, he's bigger than Marc and oh my god oh my god this is amazing, and he is so gentle and I don't know if I want him to be gentle I want him oh my god I want him to fuck me I didn't know I could feel like this…

BRANDON It's happening my God it's happening he's riding me, he's on top of me and if I don't stop him he'll make it happen too fast I want this to last I want this to be kind and loving and soft, not raw and animal the way it usually is, and so I flip him down to his back and I am on top of him and his eyes are wild and crazed and I know he wants me to just pound him, he is sweating and so am I, but I am going to take it slow and easy and make him crazy, I want this to be something special this first time because I do care about him, what is wrong with me I don't ever feel anything for anyone, but he's different he's nothing like Phil and I have to stop thinking about Phil and I have to be careful here, but I do feel something, I've not felt about anyone like this ever before, and I am kissing him again and he tastes like pot and Diet Coke but somehow it's delicious I can't get enough of him, his skin feels like satin it's firm and yet soft to the touch and he's whispering he loves me and I like hearing it, I want to say it back but I think I already did once and it doesn't matter if I do, so I say it again and I can feel him tensing up and I know he's close and I'm close and so I keep moving slowing down to make him want it even more—

DYLAN Oh my God I'm going to come and I don't want to because I don't want this to stop ever oh my God I love you Brandon I love you I love you I love OH MY GOD...

RICKY When I knocked on Brandon's door he didn't answer.

I try not to sulk about it, but I wonder why he's not there. Did he forget that I was coming by, or does he not want me to come by anymore, or what the hell is going on here and why do I care so much anyway? It's just sex, and I know that's the truth and I've always been fine with it, so why is this eating at me? I knock on Kenny's door and he's not there, either.

Where is everyone?

I text them both and stare at the screen. No answer.

Nothing.

WHERE IS EVERYONE?

PHIL Someone pounding on my door wakes me. I look at my alarm clock. Seriously? Seven in the morning?

I walk through the office and open the door. Brandon is standing there, grinning at me, holding one of those cardboard trays from Starbucks. He's grinning at me.

"What are you doing up this early?" I take one of the cups. It's a latte and it's hot and really good even if I don't want to be awake this early. Drinking it means I won't be able to go back to sleep.

Oh, well, there's things I can do, and I can get high and take a nap later.

He sits down on my bed and is still grinning at me.

"What?" I finally say.

He pats the bed beside him. "I'm here to collect on my bet. I won."

I'm not sure what he's talking about at first, and then after a moment the ridiculous grin on his face sinks in to my sleep-addled brain. "You fucked Dylan last night." I'm too sleepy and groggy to be as irritated as I should be. After that chat we had last night, I was pretty sure Dylan would never fuck Brandon.

And he's going to be insufferable about it.

He starts telling me all about it, about how he ran into Dylan in the hall and he was wasted, and he helped him to bed and didn't try anything, just got into bed with him and dozed off with him and how later Dylan woke up sober and initiated it, it was all from Dylan, and the way he's talking—

I cut him off. "It sounds like you—you have feelings for him." I raise an eyebrow. An interesting if infuriating wrinkle.

His smile fades and he narrows his eyes, thinking. "No."

"You do." I start to laugh. He hates being laughed at, I know that from years of experience dealing with his massive ego. "If you didn't, you wouldn't have had to think first. You're falling in love with that little prude."

"No."

"I can see it on your face." I'm wide awake now, and a fury is building inside me. In love with Dylan Parrish? It's like a slap in my face. "You are in love with him."

He pats the bed again. "What difference does that make? You lost the bet, and I'm here to collect."

"You can't be serious." I force myself to laugh again. "I'm not going to fuck you when you're in love with someone else, when you have feelings for someone else."

His smile fades. "I told you I don't have feelings for him."

"Oh, but you do," I tease him. "You need to break his heart now, you need to tell him it's all over, that you don't care about him and you were wrong."

"Why?"

"Why don't you want to?" Now my laughter isn't forced. "The whole point of fucking him was to make a mockery of his monogamy bullshit, wasn't it? To show him he's no better than anyone else, right? Knock him off his purity platform? So, no, you haven't really finished the job, Brandon."

A muscle in his jaw is twitching. "That wasn't the bet."

"Well, what would I have won if you hadn't?" I fold my arms. "Some bet. All I won would be not having to sleep with you. Well, it's been years and we've long agreed that we're not ever going to do that again, remember? We both agreed that we wouldn't work as a couple and we were better off as friends, remember? Your exact words were 'I wonder which one of us would cheat first.'"

I can hear the words as clearly as if he had just said them.

They weren't what I was expecting. We'd just spent a wonderful weekend together after a flirtation of about a month, and when he told me that he wasn't ready for a relationship yet and that he knew I wasn't the type either and his reputation would ruin any chances I might have for holding office in the house, it was like being slapped across the face and I just smiled back at him and said, "Of course you're right," and he kissed me and said, "I wonder which one of us would cheat first?" and I should have won an Oscar for laughing when I felt so embarrassed and humiliated, and even though I knew he was right I also had been thinking that whole weekend how much I liked him and how happy we would make each other and had actually bought into the whole happily-ever-after thing like I had before and I was never ever going to do that again, I was never going to let another man make me feel like that again.

I'd been waiting for years to say that back to him.

He flinches and stands up. "All right," he says heavily. "I'll do it."

"And be cruel."

He slams the door behind him so hard that one of my frames falls off the wall.

The bathroom door opens.

"Can I come out now?" Kenny asks.

I hold out my hands to him and nod. "How much of that did you hear?"

"Did he really bet you he could get Dylan to—"

I nod. "You know he's also been fucking Ricky?"

His face reddens.

BRANDON He opens the door and throws himself into my arms.

"When I woke up and you weren't there, I—almost started crying," he says, holding on to me for dear life right there in the hallway where anyone can see. He obviously doesn't care anymore who sees or knows about what he has done, and I know, looking down into his eyes, that even though I've convinced him that sex and love aren't the same thing, they still are in his mind, and he wouldn't have let me spend the night with him if he didn't love me.

I don't want to be loved. I don't want to love anyone.

I gently push him back inside his room and close the door. He is kissing my neck and grabbing my ass, and I take his hands off me and push him back and smile at him sadly. "Dylan, stop," I say.

He looks confused. "I—I don't understand."

"We have to pretend like last night never happened. It was a mistake."

"A mistake?" He doesn't understand, and I have never hated myself more than I do right now.

"I thought I—you know, I thought there was something there between us, and now that we've actually been together"—I can't bring myself to say *fucked*, even though I know that's the word I should use that would hurt him the most—"I know now that I don't feel that way about you. It was wrong."

He's crying now, an ugly cry with tears running down his face and snot dripping out of his nose and he's hitting me, not hard, not fighting me, but he's babbling between the sobs about how everyone was right about me and he was a fool, and I let him hit me until he isn't crying anymore and is just standing there looking at me all hurt and betrayed and I feel like I'm an idiot, an absolute idiot. Why did I let Phil do this to me, why did I let Phil make me do this? There was nothing worth it, and then I hear him laughing again and I know this is the right thing to do anyway, if I really care about Dylan the best thing to do is end this now and let him go back to his fiancé and make things right, back away, and I say good-bye and close the door behind me and walk back down the hallway and I am so angry now, I am going to make Phil pay for making me hurt him this way, and when I get to the stairs Kenny is standing there and he is angry and he shoves me into the wall and I don't know what this is about and he swings at me and I duck away from him and I don't understand and I say, "Kenny what's wrong?" and he says, "I know all about you and Ricky," and he is shouting and doors in the hallway are opening and I know it was Phil, I know Phil was the one who told him and I reach into my pocket and get out my phone and say, "I'm not the bad guy here," and I hand him my phone and he pushes me again and I say, "Check my phone, read the texts between me and Phil," and he's angry and he pushes me again and I've moved and I'm at the top of the stairs and I lose my balance—

KENNY And he falls all the way down the stairs, not rolling but straight down, and there's a loud crack when his head hits the floor at the bottom of the steps and I'm just staring down at him, and I'm aware there are other people around me, and the carpet—that's blood down there and he isn't moving.

Oh my God he isn't moving.

And the office door opens and Phil starts screaming.

PHIL Noooooooooooooooo!

RICKY Hail Mary, full of grace, the Lord is with thee, blessed art thou among women...

DYLAN No, no, no, no!

PHIL Somehow I made it through the funeral and the police and everything, and the police have ruled it an unfortunate accident and I can't believe I'm never going to see Brandon again, I can't believe he's dead and I can never say I'm sorry, I can never make it up to him.

And I know people are talking inside the house.

No one really wants to talk to me, no one will look me in the eyes.

Somehow they know, they are blaming me, but it wasn't my fault.

There's a knock on the door, and I go out and open the office door.

Kenny and Ricky and Dylan are standing there, and in Kenny's hand is Brandon's cell phone.

And I know.

They push past me into the office.

And close the door.

Kenny puts the phone down on the desk. "You need to resign the presidency today and move out. We don't care what excuse you give the brothers, you don't have to leave school or San Felice, but you are finished at Beta Kappa."

"It's your fault he's dead." Dylan sneers at me. "But as long as you go peacefully, don't put up a fight, we won't tell anyone what you really are."

They're taking turns, and there's a roaring in my ears and I know I am going to have to go, give up everything I've worked so long and so hard for, and they are saying terrible things to me and I just nod, and finally they go and take the phone with them.

I sit down at the computer and start to cry as I open the new Word document and start to type.

About the Author

Todd Gregory is a New Orleans–based writer and editor who survived Hurricane Katrina and its aftermath with the help of prescription medication. He has edited the anthologies *Rough Trade*, *Blood Sacraments*, *Wings*, *Raising Hell*, *Sweat*, and *Anything for a Dollar*. He has also published three novels and a collection of his short stories, *Promises in Every Star and Other Stories*. Todd has published short stories in numerous anthologies, and his works have been translated into German.

Books Available From Bold Strokes Books

Gatecrasher by Stephen Graham King. Aided by a high-tech thief, the Maverick Heart crew race against time to prevent a cadre of savage corporate mercenaries from seizing control of a revolutionary wormhole technology. (978-1-62639-936-5)

Wicked Frat Boy Ways by Todd Gregory. Beta Kappa brothers Brandon Benson and Phil Connor play an increasingly dangerous game of love, seduction, and emotional manipulation. (978-1-62639-671-5)

Death Goes Overboard by David S. Pederson. Heath Barrington and Alan Keyes are two sides of a steamy love triangle as they encounter gangsters, con men, murder, and more aboard an old lake steamer. (978-1-62639-907-5)

A Careful Heart by Ralph Josiah Bardsley. Be careful what you wish for...love changes everything. (978-1-62639-887-0)

Worms of Sin by Lyle Blake Smythers. A haunted mental asylum turned drug treatment facility exposes supernatural detective Finn M'Coul to an outbreak of murderous insanity, a strange parasite, and ghosts that seek sex with the living. (978-1-62639-823-8)

Tartarus by Eric Andrews-Katz. When Echidna, Mother of all Monsters, escapes from Tartarus and into the modern world, only an Olympian has the power to oppose her. (978-1-62639-746-0)

Rank by Richard Compson Sater. Rank means nothing to the heart, but the Air Force isn't as impartial. Every airman learns that rank has its privileges. What about love? (978-1-62639-845-0)

The Grim Reaper's Calling Card by Donald Webb. When Katsuro Tanaka begins investigating the disappearance of a young nurse, he discovers more missing persons, and they all have one thing in common: The Grim Reaper Tarot Card. (978-1-62639-748-4)

Smoldering Desires by C.E. Knipes. Evan McGarrity has found the man of his dreams in Sebastian Tantalos. When an old boyfriend from Sebastian's past enters the picture, Evan must fight for the man he loves. (978-1-62639-714-9)

Tallulah Bankhead Slept Here by Sam Lollar. A coming of age/coming out story, set in El Paso of 1967, that tells of Aaron's adventures with movie stars, cool cars, and topless bars. (978-1-62639-710-1)

Death Came Calling by Donald Webb. When private investigator Katsuro Tanaka is hired to look into the death of a high-profile lawyer, he becomes embroiled in a case of murder and mayhem. (978-1-60282-979-4)

The City of Seven Gods by Andrew J. Peters. In an ancient city of aerie temples, a young priest and a barbarian mercenary struggle to refashion their lives after their worlds are torn apart by betrayal. (978-1-62639-775-0)

Lysistrata Cove by Dena Hankins. Jack and Eve navigate the maelstrom of their darkest desires and find love by transgressing gender, dominance, submission, and the law on the crystal blue Caribbean Sea. (978-1-62639-821-4)

Garden District Gothic by Greg Herren. Scotty Bradley has to solve a notorious thirty-year-old unsolved murder that has terrible repercussions in the present. (978-1-62639-667-8)

The Man on Top of the World by Vanessa Clark. Jonathan Maxwell falling in love with Izzy Rich, the world's hottest glam rock superstar, is not only unpredictable but complicated when a bold teenage fan-girl changes everything. (978-1-62639-699-9)

The Orchard of Flesh by Christian Baines. With two hotheaded men under his roof including his werewolf lover, a vampire tries to solve an increasingly lethal mystery while keeping Sydney's supernatural factions from the brink of war. (978-1-62639-649-4)

Funny Bone by Daniel W. Kelly. Sometimes sex feels so good you just gotta giggle! (978-1-62639-683-8)

The Thassos Confabulation by Sam Sommer. With the inheritance of a great deal of money, David and Chris also inherit a nondescript brown paper parcel and a strange and perplexing letter that sends David on a quest to understand its meaning. (978-1-62639-665-4)